Unleashed

Book Summary

Veronica Mitchell is the epitome of success in the national and international marketing world. Her business savvy, however, could not shield her from sexual abuse, bullying, and toxic individuals who saw her as someone to manipulate. Her indomitable spirit would be her personal shield, one she would wield during every battle and embrace with every victory. Truly a story of perseverance and healing, *Unleashed* will speak to every person whose spirit and soul have been broken and ultimately reclaimed.

ISBN 978-1-54399-641-8 eBook 978-1-54399-642-5
Printed in the United States
Metaphysical, Romantic Fiction

Author: Dannet Botkin
Writer: Robin Burns

DEDICATION

This book is dedicated to all who endured bullying.

To encourage women to be powerful, ambitious, successful, and strong: *roar, lionesses, roar!*

To spread hope, love, understanding, and compassion to all suffering from heartbreaks, pain, obstacles, and emotional or physical abuse.

To invoke forgiveness even for those who are not sorry. *Release yourself from the hurt. Forgive and rise, warriors.* You've got this!

–DANNET BOTKIN

Chapter 1

Sky-High Origins

Veronica Mitchell learned at a very tender age that there would be times when she would have to look deep within herself to push past pain and adversity; to believe in her own power.

In 1972, Colorado welcomed its newest little citizen, an infant girl destined to accomplish some significant things in her life. She crawled at five months old and walked at eleven months, and her mother claimed her first words were, "I got this."

At four years old, Veronica was a petite bundle of blonde curls, round apple cheeks, and cotton-candy-pink lips. A pint-size force of nature, she was a little girl with a loving heart who charmed all she met.

Veronica enjoyed what many little girls her age enjoyed: playing with Barbie and G.I. Joe dolls, hosting exquisite little pretend tea parties, playing with her dogs, coloring, and drawing. She was a bit of a tomboy though and loved to explore the nearby forest with her friends. They spent countless hours walking across long, uprooted trees that served as balance beams and collecting pinecones, oddly shaped rocks, and various treasures that nature had left in random scatters.

Veronica had a loving family. Her mother, Laura Mitchell, was an active, intelligent, and fun woman who loved both her and her sister deeply. She would often take them for adventurous hikes into the beautiful Colorado mountain range. She would host the best birthday blasts, parties that were the makings of every little girl's dreams.

Her father, David Mitchell, was a computer systems analyst. He worked with many of the leading defense contractors, and his job required frequent travel. Veronica dearly missed her father's presence in her daily life, but she knew she was always in his heart. His beginnings had been humble, and he wanted nothing more than to ensure his daughters had the best that life could offer.

Veronica lived for the times he was home. He was playful and doting, and her entire world felt complete when she was around him. He would make the best waffles, popcorn, and treats. His attention and love were magical.

Veronica enjoyed a loving relationship with her older sister, Mia. They would often go through their daily lives as the best of friends, but as with most sisters, sibling rivalry sometimes crept into their relationship.

In addition to life near the scenic panorama of Colorado, Veronica looked forward to summer trips to Oklahoma to visit the great-uncle she lovingly called Bobo and her great-aunt Doodie. They lived on a farm with a menagerie of animals. It was here that Veronica developed her love of critters and her respect for nature and the environment. Veronica particularly loved their horses and enjoyed riding her two favorites, Bullet and Joe.

Back in Colorado, Veronica also had a great-grandmother, Gigi, whom she worshipped. Gigi was like a free-spirited unicorn/angel/flower child with a light and loving energy that emanated from her. Gigi also used to draw with Veronica. The times they spent together drawing, exchanging secrets, and just being together inspired Veronica's creativity. It was also the origin of her lifelong love of art.

The Mitchell family had a camper, and they traveled to many places in the United States. Veronica marveled at the gorgeous coastlines, majestic mountain ranges, and beautiful national parks .

When her dad had time off from work, he would rally the family and announce, "Let's pack our bags and go! Let's experience the colors, sights, and sounds of nature, and take in the beauty of this magnificent land." David Mitchell would then offer a "hip, hip, hooray," and the entire family would join in the chant.

Veronica Mitchell's young life in Colorado was not without its share of pain, however. When Mr. Mitchell was home and her parents had the opportunity to go out alone, a babysitter cared for Veronica and Mia. For most young children, a babysitter means a free pass for staying up past bedtime, junk food binges, and pillow fights.

For Veronica and Mia, just hearing the words, "Your father and I are going out tonight," made them shudder. One of the neighbors, a teenager named Marlon, was their babysitter. Marlon's agenda did not include television and late-night snacks. Marlon taught the sisters that the devil was closer than people thought.

Marlon sexually molested Veronica and Mia for almost two years. Veronica was about four years old when the abuse started. Marlon would bring Veronica into the bathroom with him and force her to perform oral sex on him. Later in the evening, it would be Marlon's turn to perform oral sex on Mia and Veronica.

Upon the discovery of the abuse by Mrs. Mitchell, Marlon was no longer their sitter. Mrs. Mitchell was shocked and heartbroken at the abuse suffered by her daughters. The mode of resolution in those days, however, was not to openly discuss matters of this nature.

Mrs. Mitchell was a woman of high morals, and she believed strongly in the sanctity of all life. She did not share their daughters' abuse by Marlon with her husband. If she had, Marlon's life would have ceased to exist.

Veronica did not understand why Marlon had abused her. She compartmentalized the fear and shame and did not walk away from the abuse unscathed. It cost her some of her childhood innocence as well as her ability to trust.

While Veronica enjoyed free-spirited play with children in the neighborhood, the antics that occurred in their locked basement was another thing she hated enduring.

She and Mia had a friend named Devin. An unkempt little boy that Veronica and the other children called Ragamuffin always accompanied Devin. Devin and Ragamuffin devised a cruel way to trick Veronica when Mrs. Mitchell was engaged in cooking, sewing, or reading a book. They would lure Veronica into the basement, then lock the door and tell her that horrible things would happen to her sister if she screamed when in the basement.

Her only way to exit from the basement was to pee in a plastic cup, knock on the basement door, and plead to be released. Once out of the basement, she would have to drink the urine in front of Devin and Ragamuffin.

The basement was always dark and smelled musty, and Veronica would make her way down the stairs toward the window to take advantage of the minimal light. She would sit cross-legged on the floor, cup her head in her hands, and wait for nature's call so she could pee in the cup.

Undoubtedly, an older child would have come up with a plan of escape, or a way to inform her parents of what was happening. However, Veronica was six years old and did not know how to extricate herself from the horrible situation.

Devin and Ragamuffin got away with their sadistic basement game three times before Mrs. Mitchell found out what was happening. David was never one of Veronica's playmates again, and luckily, the child known as Ragamuffin moved away with his family.

Veronica did have pleasurable times and the chance to make lasting, happy memories. One she would never forget occurred after camping out with Mia in her father's home office. Veronica awoke to use the bathroom, and she saw a mysterious humanlike presence surrounded by a green aura. It stopped her in her tracks, and she rubbed her eyes several times to make sure she was not seeing things, but the presence remained. Fueled by a sense of curiosity she walked closer to it, stopping several inches away from touching it. Then it spoke. "Don't worry. You are safe. It may seem that help is far away, but you will always be under my protection."

Coming of Age

Later that year, a move from Colorado to New Jersey was very tough for Veronica. The home they moved into was large, and the town was quite wealthy. Despite the upper middle-class trappings of life in New Jersey, Veronica missed the beauty of Colorado, and the animals and rustic charm of her visits to Oklahoma. And, quite unexpectedly, Veronica found herself in the unenviable position of being the target of bullies.

Veronica's mother had a love of sewing, and she applied this love to her design of long, feminine ruffle dresses for Veronica. The bullies quickly homed in on her different style of dressing and teased her. The taunting felt like sharp stabs that penetrated her skin and cut deep into her soul.

Every morning when Veronica walked the short distance to the bus stop, she was greeted with a barrage of insults: "Granny bony knees!" "Where did you find that dress?" "Raggedy Ann, where's Andy?"

She could best describe the feeling by saying that her heart hurt. The brave face she thought she was wearing neither blocked out the cruel voices nor diminished the hurt, but she had to try.

As part of her ongoing pretense not to hear, she resorted to reading books from her Nancy Drew collection. It was tough reading and walking. Sometimes she would trip over the lace hem of her long dress, and she had to steady herself to avoid falling.

Once she did fall, causing her book bag to unlatch, spilling her books and papers everywhere. Her Wonder Woman metal lunch box opened, and her apple rolled out, picking up momentum as it made its way into the street. The primary tormentors, the "poison girls" as Veronica had dubbed them, laughed so hard tears were streaming down their faces.

Veronica had a small cubbyhole that was her place of escape and her ultimate retreat. It was where her seven-year-old hands created their most profound artistic masterpieces. The cubbyhole was no more than a large niche in the wall, but when she walked into it, Veronica felt like great impenetrable walls surrounded her . She had the ability to see out, but no one could look in. *She felt safe.*

Veronica would often entertain herself by shouting, "Hark, who goes there?" to her imaginary visitors. She had the power to deny all who requested asylum in the huge fortress. "And what is your business today with Queen Veronica? Is her highness expecting you? What gifts have you to offer the queen in exchange for your entrance into her kingdom?"

Sometimes Veronica would simply sketch. The meditative and healing power of sketching was another gift that Gigi had given her. It became art therapy for Veronica, and she would use it throughout her life when she needed to acknowledge and release pain.

It was not that time stood still when Veronica was in her cubbyhole. It was as if her world were devoid of time. She was a beautiful, free-floating spirit who enjoyed that she could simply be. There were no schedules to keep, no rules to follow, no tormentors to flee.

Once the bells rang announcing the start of the school day, the tormenting continued. When the teacher called each student's name for attendance, laughter and animal sounds filled the room at the sound of Veronica's name.

Throughout the day, she was the target of spitball attacks and paper airplanes with various insults scribbled on them like "yuck" and "ugly." Even afternoon quiet time, the designated forty-five minutes when students put their heads down on their desks, was prime time for sneers and whispers, all at Veronica's expense.

Veronica's need to fit in was never more desperate than at recess. She would watch the other girls draw pink, blue, and green boxes on the sidewalk with chalk, numbering them for hopscotch. She felt particularly sad when they played the handclap games "Miss Susie" and "Say, Say, My Playmate" because she had fond memories of playing them with her great-grandmother Gigi. Gigi would always make up silly, nonsensical words that made Veronica laugh so hard she nearly cried. She missed Gigi in Oklahoma and Colorado so much at times that she thought it was more than her seven-year-old heart could take. Every day she watched her classmates play, and she was always the outsider. This caused Veronica to visit the school nurse at least two times per week.

Veronica would sheepishly stand up, smooth down her dress, and walk up to her teacher's desk. There would be a faint hum in the room, and Veronica could not tell if it was the air conditioner or the muffled laughter of her classmates as she walked to the front of the classroom.

Ms. Caffrey would be engrossed in grading her students' basic addition, subtraction, or vocabulary word assignments. Veronica had to mumble "Excuse me" a couple of times before her teacher looked up.

"What is it, Veronica?" Ms. Caffrey would ask softly.

"I would like a note to go see the nurse, please," Veronica would say, allowing her head to rise and her eyes to meet her teacher's.

Veronica always expected to see the look of impatience that was usually reserved for students who could not correctly answer a question after the teacher's lesson. Instead, Veronica would see tenderness and compassion in her teacher's round face, and the intensity of those emotions would cause Veronica's eyes to water.

"Are you okay, dear?" or "Can I help you, Veronica?" Ms. Caffrey would ask as she moved closer to Veronica.

"No, ma'am," Veronica would stammer. "My heart just hurts."

Always, Ms. Caffrey smiled softly and gestured Veronica to head to the nurse's station. Veronica held her breath, each time, as she walked slowly out of the classroom. She closed the door behind her, she felt her pace accelerate, and tears begin to moisten her cheeks as she ran to the nurse's station.

The receptionist, Ms. Beth, would faithfully peer up from her typewriter as Veronica found a seat in the lobby.

"How can I help you today, Ms. Mitchell?" she would ask cheerfully.

"I need to see the nurse, please," Veronica would state matter-of-factly.

"Be specific, Veronica," Ms. Beth would direct.

Veronica would experience a flood of panic and fear churning in her stomach, as she would struggle to say, "My heart hurts."

Beth always collected a bottle of juice from the office refrigerator, grabbed a small pack of animal crackers from the cupboard, and handed them to Veronica.

"The nurse will see you in ten minutes." Beth would say those very words to Veronica again and again for over a year.

There was no real medical reason to explain Veronica's heart pain. She was a bullied child—a child who had experienced cruelty—and that pain had to go somewhere, so it settled in her heart.

Each night Veronica would kneel at her bed, clasp her hands together, and say her prayers. After getting into bed, Veronica would listen to her mother's reassurance that her Scooby-Doo night-light really did provide enough protection from the darkness. She would exchange kisses and "I love you's" with her mother. After she closed the bedroom door, Veronica would count to seventy-five, push her covers back, and kneel on the floor against her bed for round two of her nightly prayers.

"Please, God," the blonde child would plead, "make them stop saying all those cruel things. Please, God, can I make just two friends? I promise to be good, do all my chores, and take care of any stray animals I find."

Satisfied that she had articulated her wishes clearly without being boastful or sounding selfish, Veronica would climb back into her bed.

After one particularly tough afternoon on the playground, when two of her male classmates had squirted her with small toy water guns causing her to run and fall, Veronica felt that her nightly prayers for relief and friends needed some modification. "Please God, I know you are busy, but I am kind of desperate, so one friend would be fine if you can make sure that person is really, really nice."

In time, Veronica was able to make a few friends. Marilyn and Cathy became her new confidants. Both girls were bullies, so it was quite the turnaround when the little girl bullied for so long was now hanging out with two of the bullies.

Veronica now had her first inkling of how it felt to fit in on the playground. One day when playing outside, feeling particularly vindicated and powerful, a giant eagle swooped down and almost knocked her over. It was as if the eagle thought she was mere prey, and then quickly realized she was quite the embodiment of strength. It was a memory that would remain with Veronica always.

The three girls were friends until middle school, a time when Marilyn and Cathy made a ritual of pulling tricks on Veronica that served to embarrass her. Marilyn and Cathy were not as popular as Veronica had become. Angered by this, they enjoyed pranking and bullying Veronica once again in order to maintain any kind of cool status.

By the time Veronica entered middle school, the petite blonde girl had turned into quite the stunner. Like most girls her age that were typically described as either cute or pretty, Veronica could be both. She could be femininely pretty in a little dress or be the cute tomboy.

Her best friend in high school was Amanda. The two were inseparable. They went to many concerts, among them Pink Floyd, Def Leppard, Rush, and Journey, where they drank and smoked. Once at a Grateful Dead concert, they even dropped acid. But their buzz lasted about twenty-four hours and was so freaky, they each swore they never, ever wanted to do it again.

They were "oh so pretty" ripped tights and oversized blazers talking and giggling about the boys they liked. As was the typical rebellious behavior of girls their age, they loved sneaking out of the house.

They would go into the woods and swing on vines or find a log they could sit on and share secrets and stories. They would go to make-out parties, which usually included drugs and booze. They smoked pot often (sometimes laced with coke) and loved Whip-Its. The boys were plentiful, and the parties were delicious, in part because they were like forbidden fruit.

Veronica knew she was one of the hot girls, and she knew others knew it too. It was not that she flaunted it. She just had an extra dose of self-confidence that was new to her, and it felt good.

Veronica relished her newfound appeal as she and Amanda casually spent time with boys at parties. She went as far as she wanted with them, depending on her feelings. A casual make-out date was fun, and Veronica enjoyed the power of knowing that she could take a guy to the point where he thought sex was inevitable, and then she could change her mind and pull away. Nothing beat the feeling of knowing she had the power!

When she was at home waiting for a date, she laughed to herself as she wondered what kind of message her dates received when they came to pick her up. Upon entering the Mitchell home, the first things visible were David Mitchell's large collection of guns on the wall above the staircase.

An annual event unique to New Jersey was Mischief Night. It was an informal holiday of sorts teenagers celebrated by engaging in pranks and minor vandalism. One evening resulted in the arrest of Veronica and her friends. The alcohol had flowed freely that evening, and Veronica had definitely delighted in her share while stringing toilet paper through bushes, knocking on doors then running away, and other acts of mild debauchery.

Her parents were called to pick up their daughter from the police station, and Veronica's dad, a handsome man with a compelling demeanor, arrived to bring Veronica home. There were no charges filed, and Mr. Mitchell imposed no restrictions or other punishment on Veronica. He thought that the hangover and accompanying sickness his daughter was sure to feel the next day would certainly be punishment enough.

Unapologetically Resilient

As difficult as the move to New Jersey had been, moving to Dallas, Texas proved to be equally tough. It was hard leaving Amanda, who was alternately sad and angry at Veronica's departure.

The culture of Texas was a shock to Veronica; she had been used to living in more diverse settings. She had certainly encountered her fair share of bullies, but bigots were another matter altogether.

Veronica met Chandler in her junior year of high school, and she had her first full sexual experience with him. It started out as a crush, a storm surge of electricity that was romantic and sweet, yet edgy and tense all at the same time. Even at their young age, their sexual relationship was built on mutual respect, and Veronica felt safe with Chandler.

Sex with him was exciting and passionately hot, yet extremely gentle and romantic. It was as if a Harlequin romance novel merged with *Penthouse Forum*. It was everything she had ever dreamed it could be and more. And it was just what she needed to help her dull the memories of those early experiences with Marlon.

Her sexual relationship with Chandler lasted about six months. When it ended, Veronica was not only heartbroken, she was hurt by the way Chandler started to treat her in public. Once again, Veronica had to deal with the cruelness of being bullied. This time was infinitely worse because she gave this bully her virginity.

Chandler would shout out hurtful comments in the school cafeteria, their classroom, and other public places. "Veronica is the ugliest person I have ever seen" or "I hope that ugly girl does not sit at this table."

Veronica knew on an intellectual level that he was belittling her publicly because he was a popular jock, and he needed to act like a dick to maintain his cool image. But, on an emotional level, it hurt more than she could put into words.

It was in Texas while bar hopping with friends that Veronica met Joseph. He was at a bar watching a football game. Joseph was tall, dark-haired, and very handsome. For her, it was lust at first sight. She was sure that he had also fallen for her... hard.

As easy on the eyes as Joseph was, Veronica found him to be incredibly easy to talk to, and she felt she could truly be herself with him. They enjoyed movies, listening to music in small bars and cafés, and just spending time together.

After she and Joseph dated for a few months, Veronica began attending Southwest University in Austin. She was surprised to see that Joseph was threatened by her studies. He made the decision not to attend college yet was jealous of the time she spent away and devoted to classes.

While she did not completely understand Joseph's feelings, they were in a serious and committed romantic relationship, and Veronica didn't want to lose him. Against her parents' wishes, she transferred to a college closer to Joseph in Dallas. At Texas Woman's University, she studied fashion merchandising. She eventually switched to the University of North Texas, where she graduated cum laude within three years while working three jobs.

Unfortunately, her relationship with Joseph remained strained. But Joseph no longer felt isolated. His best friend Stephen had returned to the area around the same time Veronica did, and Joseph and Stephen became inseparable. They double-dated with Stephen and his girlfriend Janelle, and the two couples got along well. On one occasion, they got along very well. Stephen had won tickets to a concert from a local radio station, and part of the package included a limo ride to the concert venue.

The champagne was flowing, inhibitions loosened, and soon clothing came off. Veronica participated in her first foursome. Perhaps due to the champagne, she was not the least bit nervous about having group sex in the limo. When she coupled with Stephen, it was amazing. It was hot. Stephen was an aggressive lover, rough but not too rough. He tugged Veronica's hair, and she felt that "you Tarzan, me Jane" feeling, and she loved it. Primitive. Primal. Pleasurable.

Veronica had never been with another woman, but she just went with it, and Janelle did the same. It was satisfying and soft in a way that sex with a man could never be. When Janelle went down on her, she suddenly felt that dicks were very overrated. She guessed that women instinctively knew what other women like. Veronica promised herself that this would not be her last time having sex with a woman.

Heartbroken and Uplifted

The ongoing tensions in Veronica and Joseph's relationship had taken their toll, and the two of them decided that they each wanted different things in life. The split was heartbreaking; they had spent five years together. Despite her pain, Veronica could honestly say that she would not have traded that time with him for anything.

Most of the time, Veronica was able to navigate through her busy days without reminders of their time together. However, when she least expected it, something seemingly insignificant would trigger a flood of memories, and she would feel consumed with grief. She was a resilient woman, but she found she needed to summon that strength to put her relationship with Joseph into context and move forward with her life.

To help 'Zen out,' Veronica would often spend late afternoons sitting alone on the edge of what she called her place of perpetual peace, a small hill overlooking Grapevine Lake in Texas. Sometimes she would meditate, and other times she would sketch. She found the solitude healing.

One day a sailboat idled up to the edge of the water, and an older man stood up from the helm. Using a megaphone, he asked her if she wanted to go for a ride. If anyone else anywhere else had done this, it would have seemed both creepy and sleazy, but this man appeared to have that... Je ne sais quoi.

"My name is Theo. I have seen you sitting there before, staring at the lake. Would you like to join me for a sail? We could sip some champagne, have some cheese and grapes. My wife died recently, and the water just seems to comfort me. Maybe you need some comfort of your own? Or maybe I am just a silly old man. Either way, I would love your company."

Veronica accepted his gracious offer, and so began the first of what was to be many sails with him. Veronica and Theo would drink champagne and dine on crab, grapes, and cheese. The water was soothing for them both, and the easy, friendly conversation was a balm that softened the hard edges of grief. Veronica referred to Theo as one of her earth angels. He would remain one of her most poignant memories of life in Texas.

Chapter 2

A Manhattan, Please

"I've been everywhere, man. I've been everywhere," Veronica sang softly to herself as she noted the signs for New Jersey/Lincoln Tunnel into New York. Veronica had been to many different places in her life thus far, criss-crossing the United States and Canada.

However, the kinship she felt with the Johnny Cash lyrics was because of the range of emotions and experiences she had endured. There were so many highs and lows. Veronica had survived the sexually abusive babysitter. Yet during that hellish year, she had enjoyed making wonderful memories with her precious great-grandmother Gigi.

Her elementary and middle school years were more difficult than they needed to be because of cruel bullies, but she not only survived those indignities, she surmounted them. She graduated cum laude and most recently secured three interviews with prestigious fashion companies in New York City. Now she was on a cross-country road trip, on her way to the Big Apple to begin a new career and start a new life.

Few young women her age got the opportunity to work on Madison Avenue, and certainly not many had been as sought after. Veronica accepted an offer from Bellissimo Sei, a company that imported lingerie from England, Holland, Italy, and France.

This chapter in her life was a realization of Veronica's dream—working for an exclusive company in a fabulous city, and on Madison Avenue, no less. It really did not get much better.

She had planned to sublease a furnished apartment through a friend of a friend. The apartment belonged to an actress, and this made her feel like she was a gorgeous city starlet.

She glanced over at her father, snoring away against a pillow propped up against the passenger side window. She was grateful that he offered to travel with her to New York. While Veronica loved adventure, the prospect of driving to Manhattan alone seemed a bit daunting.

She knew her dad was proud of her. He had told her that often. During the trip, he asked her questions about her new job, but not just the socially polite inquiries about how many people worked there or if she could pack a lunch to save money. David Mitchell wanted to know if his daughter had given thought to how she would develop marketing strategies at the company. He also shared her enthusiasm about traveling to Paris, England, Amsterdam, and other exciting destinations.

Veronica remembered how her father constantly implored her to do her best with her studies in high school and college. Mr. Mitchell was very ambitious and driven. He was a self-made man who knew that success was attainable through focus and hard work.

He also knew that it would be more difficult for his daughter to succeed. Gender roles and views on equality between the sexes had changed dramatically since he was his daughter's age, but bias and sexism were still alive and well. He believed that a superior education and a tough-as-nails work ethic would be Veronica's protection against those who may wish to diminish her because she was a woman.

Now he was with her, sharing a road trip that would be the start of the rest of her life. It would be an important first step in the grabbing of the proverbial brass ring. She would be that much closer to the culmination of success. She would be at that place where education shook hands with sheer determination, and asked street smarts and a splash of good luck to come along with them for the ride for good measure.

Mr. Mitchell was very impressed with Veronica's apartment, almost as impressed as Veronica was! It was larger than she expected, but still maintained a funky, bohemian charm. Veronica felt a poignant rush of nostalgia when she noticed a small niche in the bedroom with long sequined beads covering the entrance. How she loved her little niches—she knew this was where she would have her most creative inspirations.

That first night in New York City, Veronica and her dad found a great little Italian eatery that served the most delicious pizza. Veronica had missed that greatly from her days in Jersey. The pizza, the cozy atmosphere of the restaurant with soft candles on every table, and the fragrant bouquet of Chianti made for a nice buzz on an increasingly cold New York evening.

The two walked back to her apartment, and it was snowing. The weatherman on the local news predicted scattered snow flurries, and Veronica prepared for the chilly morning ahead by setting out a warm and stylish outfit for her first day of work. She was in bed by 9:30 p.m. and hoped to have a refreshing night of sleep.

She awoke to her alarm at 6:00 a.m. and to the smell of freshly brewed coffee. She found her dad staring out the window of the nineteenth-floor apartment. "What's up?" Veronica asked, savoring her first sip of morning inspiration.

"It's more about what's down," Mr. Mitchell said, "about four feet of snow."

They listened to the news and heard that local state government offices were closed, schools were closed, and LaGuardia and JFK Airports were closed, with Newark being the only airport open with very limited flights.

Veronica did not receive a "we are closed" phone call and she wanted to make a positive impression on her first day, so Veronica promptly showered, put on her snow boots, and got ready to walk to work.

When she checked in at the lobby security desk of the twelve-story building, she was informed the office suites of Bellissimo Sei would be closed for business that day.

Trekking back home in the snow, she was both excited and disappointed. She was disappointed because she was eager to start her new job. Her excitement came from the prospect of building a snowman with her dad, a pleasure she had not outgrown.

The snow continued that afternoon and evening, and when it had stopped, New York City was blanketed by about sixteen inches of snow.

Veronica did not work the next day, and Mr. Mitchell could not find a flight home due to the inclement weather. More snow hit the city for three additional days. Mr. Mitchell finally booked a flight home twelve days after arriving to the Upper West Side with his daughter.

During his stay, Veronica was troubled by consistent nightmares of something happening to her father. Several nights in succession, she had dreams of his death. The fear that the dreams were a harbinger of things to come was a feeling that Veronica could not shake. She found herself constantly asking her father how he felt or if he was too tired to venture out on their evening trek for dinner. Despite constant reassurances from him, Veronica could not put her mind at ease.

Throughout her life, Veronica Mitchell had been an empath. This made her highly attuned to the emotions and energy of people in her life, as well as strangers she would meet. She would experience the emotions of others as if they were her own.

It was often painful for Veronica, as she became a human sponge—absorbing the pain and stress of others. As an empath, she was sharply intuitive and adept at reading people and situations beyond just surface-level impressions. Veronica also had a sincere giving nature, and she genuinely wanted to heal people who were experiencing pain.

She stressed while her father's flight was en route but was finally able to both exhale and end her pacing when she got the call from her mother that he had arrived safely in Texas.

"Yes, dear, he's understandably tired. It was a long flight, but he is fine."

Veronica was relieved but needed to unwind. She prepared a hot bubble bath, opened a bottle of red wine she had purchased from a trendy little market off Madison Avenue, and settled in for a long, relaxing soak.

Feeling completely tranquil, Veronica relaxed into her bed with a fashion magazine and a book. She thumbed through only a few pages of the magazine before dozing off. She was awakened by the sound of the phone ringing at 3:07 a.m. Her hand trembled as she put the receiver to her ear.

"Sweetheart, your dad is in the hospital," Laura Mitchell said calmly. "He passed out in the shower. The doctors said that he lost seventy percent of his blood due to a bleeding ulcer. He will need to remain in the hospital a week or so for observation, then he can go home. We are so lucky this happened at home and not on that airplane."

As she listened to her mother tell her that her father would be fine, and that it was not necessary for her to come home, Veronica felt an eerie chill cloak her. She realized that her dreams about her father's death almost became a reality. This was not the first time she had a premonition. It would not be the last.

A few nights after that, Veronica was sitting in her living room watching television when she heard a sound outside the front door. It sounded like someone trying to break in the neighbor's door. She glanced toward the front door and saw the knob moving. She then saw the front door open, and a hand emerged, straining to undo the chain lock.

Veronica ran to the kitchen and grabbed a rolling pin. She ran to her front door and began hitting the hand repeatedly. She heard a muffled male scream, then the sound of someone running down the stairs.

Walking back to the kitchen, Veronica reflected on what had just happened. *I just fought off a potential would-be intruder/burglar/rapist with a rolling pin. Guess I really am a true New Yorker.*

Over the next few weeks, Veronica settled in nicely at Bellissimo Sei. She had been eager to work with her new boss, Piera Conti, who was the owner of the company. Bellissimo Sei was regarded as one of the largest haute couture lingerie importers in the United States. Piera and Bellissimo Sei had each exceeded Veronica's expectations. Piera was a consummate professional who knew the fashion industry inside and out. She was as chic as the day was long, and she had more personal style than a snowy winter night had bluster. Veronica knew she would learn much from her.

Piera loved to dress in only the most stylish clothes from only the best designers. She loved and sought out luxurious cuisine, rich furnishings, and exquisite men. She strove to surround herself with only the best people. Piera's keen eye for detail and superb instincts enabled her to recognize quality in a sexy undergarment or talent in an employee. She sized up Veronica Mitchell as a talented young woman who was poised and ambitious with a bright future ahead of her.

As this was Veronica's first job working for an international wholesale company, Piera could not justify paying her a high-end salary. So as additional compensation, Piera purchased Veronica's wardrobe for her. She honestly had a fondness for the young woman, but she also wanted to ensure her director of sales and marketing was attired in only the best apparel. Piera saw Veronica as a reflection of herself and wanted her to look the part of someone who worked for her.

As a director at Bellissimo Sei, Veronica had the opportunity to travel frequently for meetings, trade shows, and other specific marketing or operations projects.

Veronica had a wonderfully eccentric coworker named Lidiya who did her part to ensure that the stresses of high-end wholesale did not get the best of the talented team at Bellissimo Sei.

On Veronica's first day, Lidiya gently knocked on Veronica's door, saying softly, *"Vpusti menya. Vpusti menya."*

Veronica hesitated for a few moments, unsure of how to proceed. Veronica's ear was pressed firmly against the rich mahogany grain door, and from the other side, Veronica heard Lidiya say, "It means, 'Let me in. Let me in.'"

When Veronica opened the door, Lidiya greeted her affectionately, kissing both cheeks. "Lady, where have you been all my life?" Lidiya broke into an impromptu torch song, giving it her best Marilyn Monroe impersonation:

"Thank you, Ms. Veronica, for all the things you will do. Thank you, Ms. Veronica, a great big welcome to you."

Lidiya grabbed her crotch when she said the word *big* and swiveled her hips from side to side in the gesture of a man urinating. Lidiya then blew Veronica a big, exaggerated kiss and ran her hands down her body, caressing her curves á la Marilyn. Veronica stood by, laughing so hard she tasted the salt of her tears when they ran down her lips.

So began a strong working relationship that was always lively and filled with the unexpected. Lidiya was the sales representative for Russian and French vendors. And, because of Lidiya, Veronica got to spend time in the Russian enclave of New York City and experienced Russian culture in food, drink, and dance.

Veronica appreciated having a Russian friend and colleague. It was truly lifesaving. Veronica supervised a salesperson in Dallas who once processed an order from a customer who was part of the Russian mob, but she was unaware of their identity and notoriety.

One morning on an otherwise typical day in the world of high-end lingerie, Veronica responded to a knock on the door. Two imposingly large men donned in expensive suits and armed with equally imposing automatic weapons greeted her. They were representing their cronies who were eagerly expecting their fancy intimate apparel order. After all, nothing says mobster mistress like amethyst-colored silk, lace garter belts, and push-up bras. There had been a delay with the delivery date because of logistics, but that had not been communicated to the Russian buyers.

Fortunately, Lidiya was able to explain what had happened in her most colorful native Russian tongue. After her detailed analysis of the situation, Lidiya and the men were laughing and sharing stories.

Naughty Arabian Nights

Veronica had met a handsome Lebanese man named Gannon at a bar after a fashion trade show. Remembering Piera emphatically teaching her that every woman needs to have at least one rich, tall, dark, and mysterious man in her life… Gannon definitely fit the bill.

Gannon was an investment banker at Citibank who had lots of disposable income and did not mind spending it on dates with Veronica. They dined at exclusive New York City restaurants and enjoyed the best nightlife that the city had to offer.

Gannon may have worked in a conservative industry, but he was an ardent and imaginative lover away from the office. Veronica and Gannon had risqué sex on the rooftop of his building, on his balcony overlooking Park Avenue, in elevators, on stairs, on the hoods of expensive cars, and just about everywhere else when the mood struck.

Gannon and Veronica had a wonderful relationship that lasted about a year. Their romance began to unravel right around the time that Veronica went on an Alaskan cruise with her aunt Nena. Nena was unable to get around without the aid of a wheelchair, so she invited her favorite niece to accompany her on the bucket-list cruise. They saw the glaciers and went whale watching, and Veronica lived her dream of gliding over the vast, breathtakingly beautiful Alaskan landscape in a seaplane.

During the days, Veronica would spend time with Nena, and then evenings were spent on her own. She won a disco-dancing contest, partied with some of the staff (including the captain, who flirted with her), and had an overall fabulous time. Veronica viewed the cruise as one of her best adventures.

Unfortunately, during the cruise, Veronica received an urgent message that Gannon was trying to contact her.

When Veronica finally spoke with Gannon, he told her that her friend Marlo, who had partied with Veronica, Gannon, and his friends twice when she had visited Veronica, had contacted him and said that Veronica wanted to break up with him. Marlo also told him that Veronica never wanted to hear his voice again or have any contact whatsoever with him. Gannon just wanted to know why and was confused about why Veronica did not tell him personally.

Veronica had to explain to Gannon that she was very happy with their relationship and had no desire to end it. She explained away Marlo's actions as jealousy over Veronica's success.

When Veronica returned from the cruise, it seemed as though things were not the same between Gannon and her. She attributed it to the stress of the misunderstanding caused by Marlo and assumed that everything would smooth over eventually. They still had fun and enjoyed nights on the town, but there was an underlying tension.

Shortly after her return, Gannon informed Veronica that he had to make a trip to Lebanon to help his parents with a family matter. He expected to be gone for about ten days. He promised that upon his return, they would go to dinner at the place of her choice, go out dancing, and then spend a romantic weekend in bed.

While Gannon was in Lebanon, Veronica worked and went out with friends and colleagues in the evening. One evening she went out with two of her buyers who were visiting from Dallas, and the three of them had a blast. It was a Wednesday evening, ladies' night, which meant cheap drinks for women, but it also meant guys trying to snag a cheap date.

Veronica and her friends found a bar that had the front doors open so that you could see the band playing. Veronica thought they sounded amazing and suggested they go in. There were no high-top tables with stools available, and the bar was packed. They found a place to stand near the middle of the bar, where they could still see the band and have a conversation without shouting.

One of the servers handed Veronica a pretty, coral-colored drink and explained, "Here's an Alabama Slammer from that lady over at the bar."

At first, Veronica felt a twinge of disappointment that the sender was not a man. The feeling puzzled her. She was not in the market to meet anyone; she was definitely happy in her relationship with Gannon. However, a little extra male attention was always good for the ego.

Veronica glanced toward the woman, held the drink up, and smiled, gesturing a thanks. The woman sauntered her way toward Veronica, heads turning as she moved. As she got closer, Veronica saw that the woman was a dead ringer for Michelle Pfeiffer. Drop-dead gorgeous. Veronica felt like she was in a movie, pursued by a mysterious, beautiful stranger.

When they were standing within two feet of each other, Veronica spoke first. "Thanks for the drink. Any significance in you sending me an Alabama Slammer?" Veronica hoped she did not sound as tongue-tied as she thought she did. "I'm drinking beer."

"Well," the woman began, "it has gin, Southern Comfort, amaretto, and orange juice. What's not to like in that cocktail? And it is not frequently ordered. When I ask for one, bartenders have to check their mixology books."

The stunning beauty continued, "Kids in the South used to drink it on spring break. And I am from Alabama, making the drink cooler. So, there you have it. Too many reasons not to enjoy something that tastes so good and looks so pretty. By the way, my name is Harper."

"Oh, wow, that is unusual and beautiful," Veronica said, mesmerized by Harper's graceful voice and flawless diction.

"Thanks," Harper said with a gracious smile. "Not that unusual. My parents and I are University of Alabama alumni, as was my favorite author, Harper Lee."

"Hmm," was all Veronica could muster. If there was anything more beautiful than Harper's face, it was her voice. It was smooth and sweet with a texture that lingered, like caramel, mixed with a dash of something not quite so innocent, like bourbon.

"I would like to kiss you," Harper said suddenly.

Veronica felt a flutter of feelings ranging from joy to confusion, regret, excitement... and yes, arousal.

Veronica blurted out her response: "I just can't. I am so very flattered, but I am in a relationship, and I am not gay." She immediately wanted to take the words back or at the very least sound as provocative and compelling as Harper.

Harper studied her face a few moments before responding, "Okay, I get that. However, a kiss is a gift of passion from the heart. Is your life so overflowing with passion that you cannot accept more?"

Veronica was speechless. Harper reached over and kissed her gently on each cheek, then once on the lips. She tasted like soft, sweet taffy, with a hint of mint. And Veronica swore she smelled the subtle scent of magnolia.

"Life does take some funny twists and turns, doesn't it?" With that, she walked away.

Veronica spent a few moments looking for her friends and found them engaged in a conversation with others. She walked over and joined in but glanced over her shoulder periodically to catch a glimpse of Harper, engaged in her own conversation with two men and a woman. All were attractive and stylish. They were each smiling and looked to be completely enchanted with the beautiful woman from Alabama. When Veronica left the bar an hour later, she felt a bit bittersweet and more than just a tad melancholy.

That night, Veronica received a call from Gannon. His voice sounded stressed and tired. He asked her if she could call his boss and tell him that he needed to stay in Lebanon for another two weeks. He had been trying unsuccessfully to contact his boss, but there were problems with phone reception, and he just needed to get the message to him. Sensing his distress, Veronica happily agreed to make the call. She assured him she would call first thing in the morning. She told Gannon not to worry and that she would handle it.

"What did I ever do to deserve you?" Gannon asked.

Veronica just felt that it was what people in relationships did. They supported each other. "Aw, anytime, hon," Veronica said sincerely.

Gannon responded, "Thank you, that is so sweet," then hung up.

Veronica was a bit taken back. She really expected a bit more gratitude or emotion from Gannon. She shrugged and attributed his less-than-romantic response to whatever family stress he was experiencing.

The next day, as promised, Veronica was able to speak to Gannon's boss, who asked that Veronica convey his and Citibank's support to him.

Sleep did not come easy for Veronica that night. She could not shake the feeling that something not quite on the level was going on with Gannon in Lebanon. The days passed by slowly, but Veronica did have the distraction of her first trip to Paris for a fashion show, and it was extraordinary.

Veronica met up with Gannon's cousin, who was more than happy to show her around Paris. Veronica cried upon seeing the Eiffel Tower because of its beauty. It was one of the most mesmerizing and compelling sights she had ever seen. Paris quickly became one of her favorite cities.

When Gannon finally arrived back, he seemed a bit distracted for the first few days, but Veronica thought that was not unusual given he had been gone almost a month. Veronica was just happy to resume their relationship, even though Gannon had still not told her what the crisis was in Lebanon that required him to stay longer.

She had asked him several times what had happened in Beirut, twice during dinners out, once after sex, and at least a half dozen other times they were together, watching television or walking the streets.

Finally, one morning over coffee, she blurted out, "I have been patient, Gannon; you have to tell me what happened in Lebanon."

He put down his *Wall Street Journal* and said, "You're right, and you have been patient." He took her hands in his, winked at her, and said, "My parents arranged a marriage for me. I have a new wife, and she will be coming here in about two weeks. I am glad we will have some time to spend together before she arrives. Please do not worry. This is not the end. We can find a way to make this work." Gannon winked at her again.

Stunned, Veronica just sat there for a few moments. Then, in a surprisingly calm way, the words came to her. "Gannon, I really want to make sure I choose my words carefully as they will have great implications for our future. So, here goes... fuck you, asshole—get out of my apartment."

Gannon just stared for a moment and then reached for his coffee cup, but Veronica placed her hand on the cup and said, "Stop. Just leave. Go."

Veronica sat for at least an hour after Gannon left. As much as she had enjoyed the time she spent with Gannon, she was more angry than sad. She did not blame herself for falling for the wrong guy, being naive, or any of the other ninety-nine things that women blame themselves for. She just knew one thing: Gannon was a dick. She was grateful she did not agree to combine their finances for investment purposes as he had suggested weeks before.

The breakup with Gannon put her in a reflective mood. She was feeling a bit vulnerable, a bit homesick, and a bit raw. Tonight, she would employ Gigi's technique for serenity and restoration: a hot bath, cool drink, sketching, and opera music. Tomorrow she would be good as new.

Despite some painful and frustrating detours along the way, New York City seemed to have welcomed Veronica Mitchell warmly. She was making friends and beginning to make a name for herself. Exposure to this completely new culture had been both exhilarating and exhausting. There were more experiences to come—and Veronica awaited them all with open arms.

Chapter 3

A New York Minute

New York City appealed to Veronica's artistic and creative nature. The Upper East Side, where her new apartment was located, had its own unique blend of folksy Bohemians mixed with the power elite, and Veronica loved walking through the Manhattan neighborhood she now called home.

One evening, exhausted after a late return from a business trip, Veronica awakened to the sound of a loud noise on the balcony. Her windows were open so she could get relief from the heat. Apartments located in old brownstones in New York City tended to be hot as the heat rose toward the top of buildings.

When she walked out to investigate the cause of the noise, she found herself face-to-face with one of NYPD's finest. Veronica could not make eye contact with the officer because she was too busy staring at the revolver pointed at her face.

She somehow had the presence of mind to ask him what was going on, and he replied that there had been a report of a break-in. When he saw the curtains blowing from the open window of her balcony, he became suspicious and began investigating.

Veronica reassured him there was no one else there, but in the interest of safety, he checked her apartment before joining his fellow officers in the search for the culprit.

Veronica stood on her balcony overlooking the city and imagined that many people would have been unnerved at what had just happened. Strangely enough, Veronica felt very safe. Whether it was a stroll down Madison Avenue, a great meal at a trendy restaurant, barhopping with friends, and yes, even a strange encounter with a gun-wielding cop, this was New York City, and Veronica Mitchell had never felt so alive!

Sexy Tour Guide

One of the positive outcomes of Veronica's relationship with Gannon was meeting Jake. Jake traveled in the same circle of friends that Gannon did, and it made sense that he would be a wonderful person to show Veronica around Paris on her next business trip.

Jake was a gorgeous Lebanese Frenchman who was also an investment banker, and when he and Veronica met, they hit it off instantly. She met him during her second business trip to Paris. He showed her all the spectacular attractions that Paris had to offer on foot and by motorbike—the Louvre, Champs-Élysées, Sacré-Cœur, Place de la Concorde, the Love Lock Bridge, Montmartre, Notre-Dame. Veronica took in all the exotic and historic sights, and each one mesmerized her.

One night while strolling around the magnificence of the city, they dined at the well-known Buddha-Bar Restaurant, located on Rue Boissy d'Anglas. Then they walked in the city some more. They had stopped to absorb the beauty on a corner under the old streetlights when Jake kissed her. For Veronica, it was one of those kisses that inspired poetry, song lyrics, and romantic movies with dashing leading men and exquisite leading ladies.

The kiss obviously rocked Jake's world as well, since he booked a room for them at the fabulous and ritzy InterContinental Hotel. They had sex in a huge bubble-filled jetted tub while they enjoyed expensive appetizers and a bottle or two of premium champagne. Overall, the evening cost $5,000, and Veronica would always remember it as one of her best dates ever.

Jake and Veronica had a great romance. They went to Madrid and hit all the hot spots. They traveled to Ronda, a beautiful mountaintop city in Spain's Málaga province dramatically set above a deep gorge known as El Tajo. It was breathtaking enough that Hemingway wrote about it in *The Sun Also Rises*.

They went to Seville, the capital of southern Spain's Andalusia region. The region is famous for flamenco dancing, as well as the Alcázar castle complex and the Plaza de Toros de la Maestranza building. Veronica found it nothing short of stunning.

They spent New Year's Eve together in Paris. In Venice, they explored and rode in a gondola. Veronica had to pinch herself to make sure she was not dreaming.

The only thing missing, the only thing that kept their relationship from being the kind of story that made for epic romance novels was the simple and unavoidable fact that Veronica was not in love with Jake, and she just was not sexually attracted to him. God knows she tried to be... God knows she willed it to be. It just was not meant to be.

One of the saddest things in Veronica's life was when she finally had to tell Jake that there would never be anything more for them than the great friendship they had created and nurtured.

Jake moved to London shortly after Veronica put the brakes on their romantic future, but he called her on and off, and she helped him perfect his English CV so he could land his dream job at JPMorgan Chase. To Veronica's delight, Jake seemed genuinely content with his new life.

Veronica was surprised when she received tickets from Jake to fly to London for a week. She missed Jake and she did want to see him again, but she was afraid that a visit would give him false hope about their future.

She called him and told him she would love to visit, but that it did not change her feelings about their friendship. Jake reassured her that he understood, and that the only thing Veronica needed to worry about was packing her suitcase and boarding that plane.

Jake was waiting for her at Heathrow Airport. Veronica was so happy to see him. Jake looked great—tan, fit, and relaxed. She hoped that he had moved on and had started dating, maybe even found that lucky girl that was the one. The thought of him with another woman made her smile, but she also felt a twinge of sadness for what could never be—that he would never be the one for her.

"Hope you're hungry," Jake said after they exchanged prolonged hugs and cheek kisses.

"Yes!" Veronica exclaimed, eager to sit down to a good meal and catch up with him.

The restaurant was a superb choice, but then Jake was a man of taste. The conversation was spirited and easy; their exchanges did not carry any hints of strain.

After brandy and a yummy trifle like dessert, Jake told her that he was eager to play tour guide again, and he had a place that she absolutely needed to see. They drove for about twenty minutes on the highway before turning onto a scenic back road. The small neighborhood was home to charming, well-manicured cottages that inspired feelings of warmth and serenity. Jake pulled into a shrub-lined driveway, up to a medium-size brick cottage that looked like a Bavarian gingerbread house. It was stunning, and Veronica fell in love with it immediately.

Jake enthusiastically opened her car door, and dropping to one knee, he exclaimed, "I don't have a diamond ring to offer as a symbol of my love, but I do have this house. Veronica, I bought this house for you, for us. Will you marry me?"

Veronica was speechless. Jake saw her hesitation, grabbed her hand, and walked her to the front door. He picked up a key hidden behind a flowering shrub and escorted her inside. The house was as charming and cozy on the inside as it appeared on the outside. Each room was clean and designed with Mediterranean decor, one of Veronica's favorites.

That did not change the fact that she was not in love with its buyer, and once again, she had to set Jake straight about where they stood.

He smiled sadly and then added, "I have time, Veronica, and I have an abundance of patience. I'll wait for you; I know you will change your mind."

The rest of her stay in London was fun filled, including a tour of the entire city by motorcycle. But there was an air of melancholy that permeated their time together.

When he drove Veronica to the airport for her return trip home, he kissed her on both cheeks and said simply, "I will wait."

Veronica cried on the flight home. She cried because there could never be a romantic future with this wonderful man, but also because she was afraid their friendship would end.

In the weeks, then months that followed, the phone calls from Jake and texts they exchanged dwindled considerably. Eventually they only exchanged birthday wishes and an occasional phone call that, sadly, seemed almost obligatory.

After a year, Jake sent her an email saying he had met someone he really cared for and planned to marry her. The news was bittersweet for Veronica, but she was happy for her dear friend. She hoped that his wife would enjoy living in the beautiful Bavarian house—the house he had bought for her.

Mystery Man and Great Betrayal

Veronica's job continued to take her to beautiful and exotic places. She was on a business trip in Cádiz, Spain, when she first spotted a handsome man at the table next to hers during lunch. No words were spoken; the two just locked eyes.

Months later, she attended a Garth Brooks concert in New York City with some friends when she saw the image of a man on the big-screen television.

"I know that guy," Veronica said softly, and it took her a few moments to remember their eye lock in Cadiz. Veronica felt strangely exhilarated after seeing his face. After all, she had seen him twice. *What were the odds of that in this world? Who is this guy?* She thought it must be fate.

Veronica carried the image of the stranger's face with her throughout the evening. It was a wonderful night. The concert was great, she was hanging with friends, and they were young, alive, and in Central Park! Veronica could not help but feel that the world was her oyster.

Some of Veronica's friends with her lived in Jersey so they planned to stay at her apartment. The drinks were flowing, conversation was warm, and the fun was overflowing. Veronica took it all in—and closed her eyes as she tried to commit an image of the evening to memory. It was a magical night. She had no idea things would turn dark.

Veronica shared a few kisses with one of her Jersey friends named Tim. They were both drunk, and other friends were engaging in random displays of affection, absolutely PG-rated stuff.

Veronica let four friends sleep in her bed, and she slept on the floor near Tim. In the middle of night, Tim got on top of Veronica and started kissing her. Veronica was half-asleep and in a near-dream state, so she was passively kissing back.

She started to roll over when Tim ripped off her pants, and before she knew it, he was inside her. Veronica's protests of "No, no, stop!" were loud enough to rouse all her friends.

They were all in the same somewhat drunken, half-asleep, and half-conscious state, so no one came to her aid. Tim had her pinned down, and despite her repeated protests and attempts to get free, he finished inside her. It was date rape. She had been violated, and it was something she would never forget.

Avant-Garde to Corporate

Veronica had been extremely successful in her role as director of sales and marketing at Bellissimo Sei. Her boss, Piera, sang her praises every day, calling her *la mia brillante dea*, Italian for "my brilliant goddess."

Veronica's business prowess had landed Bellissimo Sei a contract with a well-known fashion brand for an intimate apparel licensing deal. Veronica wrote the contract, and as usual, her innate sense of business acumen hit the mark perfectly. However, in the days and weeks that followed, she observed that the contract was not being managed the way she thought best. She felt her company was moving too quickly to maintain quality and control. Veronica knew from experience that attention to every detail was imperative for success.

This left her with a sense of dissatisfaction with the fashion world, and she felt emboldened to jump headfirst into another venture—the world of investment banking. Veronica was one of those fortunate few who was equally adept at left-brain and right-brain talents. She had a head for numbers and a mind for creativity. A sojourn into the financial world seemed a logical choice. It had certainly served her former amore Gannon well, as he had made tons of money.

Veronica always embraced opportunities for learning, and she decided that she would pursue an MBA in business and economics. Simultaneously, she started working as an administrative assistant at SIF, a well-known multinational investment bank and financial services company. The pace was hectic, and the challenges were daily, but she was in her element. A frenzied pace or chaotic structure did not discourage Veronica in the least.

Veronica trusted her professional instincts and felt that SIF was where she needed to be at this point in her career. She felt she had a lot to offer them. Certainly, those who knew Veronica Mitchell well knew that the banking community would only benefit by her becoming the latest addition to their industry.

Italian Adonis

In addition to the wonderful experiences with Bellissimo Sei and the invaluable lessons she had learned from Piera Conti, Veronica had also discovered that the fashion world seemed to be as filled with exotic men as it was spectacular clothing. Lorenzo, a very handsome Italian man from Milan, was a charter member of the exotic male club.

He walked up to her at a fashion show, introduced himself, and said, "I have had my eye on you for a long time. I have wanted to ask you out but was not sure how to. So, here goes..."

Lorenzo took a deep breath, for effect undoubtedly—it was effective—but Veronica was convinced that he did so because it also gave him time to gaze into her eyes to see if he had mesmerized her—he had.

He continued, "Ms. Veronica Mitchell, will you please have dinner with me?"

Veronica had not wanted to appear too eager, and as she had enjoyed her fair share of male suitors since her arrival in New York, she was not desperate, so her intent had been to respond matter-of-factly. She had braced herself to accept graciously, but instead blurted out, "Oh, of course, yes, you're gorgeous. Yes, let's go out."

Seriously, V, her inner cool girl voice said, *that was matter-of-fact? Why don't you just throw yourself at his feet?*

The following weekend, they enjoyed dinner at a fabulous steak house. Everything was perfect—the meal, the wine, the company. They went back to Lorenzo's incredibly trendy apartment in SoHo, where they enjoyed more wine, and that eventually led to sex.

During this time, Veronica was still completing her coursework for an MBA in business and economics, and she was still working full-time as an administrative assistant. Lorenzo had been wonderfully supportive; he would cook delicious gourmet meals for her on many weeknights. On the weekends, they would dine at trendy and delicious restaurants in New York.

The relationship thrived and was magical until Lorenzo decided to drop hints about his more adventurous sexual side. Fully listening to her inner cool girl voice this time, she vetoed his suggestion of anal sex. It simply did not appeal to her at all.

As he was denied one avenue of opportunity, Lorenzo apparently thought it was his right to explore another. He wanted to engage in oral sex. Specifically, during one of their evenings at his apartment, he wanted to go down on her. It was something she disliked, an understandably natural result of the early sexual abuse she had suffered at the hands of Marlon, the babysitter from hell.

Veronica gritted her teeth, and images of the abuse inflicted upon her by Marlon ran through her mind. And even though she gave Lorenzo an emphatic "no" to this act she found so vile and disgusting, except for the time in the limo with another woman, he did not stop.

When it was over, she threw her dress on, poured another glass of wine, and gazed at the view of the city from Lorenzo's balcony. A few moments later, when he joined her on the balcony, she turned to look at him and said, "When I say no, it means no. I do not have to shout it, I do not have to sing it, and I do not have to utter the words in three different goddamn languages . . . no is no."

Lorenzo was very apologetic, tripping over himself with loving gestures directed at Veronica. After much soul searching, she accepted his invitation for dinner a few nights later. Once again, they had an amazing rendezvous followed by visits to a few bars. Two of the bars were gay bars, popular and fun haunts for patrons of all lifestyles, so Veronica thought this bar-hopping venture was fun.

While enjoying a round of drinks at the second bar, a striking young man walked over and gave Lorenzo a kiss on the cheek and a dozen red roses. Lorenzo introduced him as Brad, thanked him graciously, and whispered in Veronica's ear that he wanted to say hello to some of his and Brad's mutual friends.

Veronica entertained herself by talking to some of the guys at the bar for the hour or so that Brad and Lorenzo were gone. She glanced over her shoulder just in time to see Lorenzo and Brad kissing affectionately. Then they walked toward the back of the bar, fading into the crowd.

When he finally came back, Veronica said, "This won't work. I am not bisexual. Sorry, honey. It just does not work for me. I hope you find a person who can share this aspect of your life with you, on your terms."

Twisted Surprises

Through mutual friends in both the fashion and banking industries, Veronica became friends with an attractive and engaging Lebanese woman named Noura. Noura was a display designer for a Bellissimo Sei competitor, Coeur.

Noura was very talented and earned the respect of her colleagues, but she had a difficult personal life. Her husband was bipolar, and Veronica never completely understood if he had found the medication that would help him or if he was just not medication compliant. It made for a tough dynamic for Noura, who assumed most of the responsibility of raising the couple's young daughter, Ariana.

Veronica valued her friendship with Noura and genuinely liked Ariana, so she was happy to help Noura by watching Ariana when Noura had errands or had work-related obligations. Sometimes if Veronica stayed late watching the toddler, or if she and Noura spent a late evening at Noura's apartment smoking a hookah, Veronica would spend the night rather than take the subway. Noura lived in a small three-bedroom apartment, and her husband would often spend the night in the upstairs office for privacy and the convenience of sleeping where he worked.

This would mean the two women would share a large bed, which Veronica did not think was unusual. Women often shared beds in dorms, during family vacations, or when visiting friends; it simply was not anything that seemed out of the ordinary.

One night, after they had stayed up late talking, nibbling on pita dipped in baba ghanoush, and drinking wine, they turned in for the evening. Almost drifting off to sleep, Veronica was startled when she felt Noura's arms embracing her. When she turned over, Noura tried to kiss her, in a decidedly not-just-friends manner. Veronica bolted upright, and as gently as she could, she told Noura she loved her as a friend, but that was as far as their relationship would ever go. Noura expressed her romantic love for her, to which Veronica replied that they should get some sleep and talk about it in the morning.

Veronica woke up to an empty apartment, a carafe of hot coffee, and some fresh pastries on the kitchen table. There was a note placed next to the carafe that read, "Sorry for last night. I clearly misread what was going on with us. I thought we were growing closer. I am taking two weeks off from work and going to visit my friends in Philly. I hope we can talk about things when I return. Love, (as a friend) Noura."

Noura did return in two weeks, but she and Veronica never met to discuss what had happened. They scheduled dates to meet, but one or the other canceled or rescheduled numerous times. The friendship subsequently fizzled as Noura divorced and then moved back to Lebanon with Ariana.

Approximately six months after moving, Noura came back. She appeared on Veronica's doorstep by surprise. When Veronica opened the door, Noura got down on one knee and asked Veronica to marry her. Veronica kindly declined the proposal. Sadly, they never spoke again.

Attractor of Broken Birds

Veronica met another man in New York named Jordan. They started out as friends, simply enjoying each other's company, hanging out together over pizza or a few glasses of wine. Soon, they began dating. Since he lived in Dallas, Veronica would stay with him when she was in the city for work, and he with her when he came to New York. In addition to enjoying each other's company, they enjoyed a mutually satisfying sexual relationship.

Jordan had an infinite sadness about him. He had inherited a large sum of money from his father's estate. His father was killed when a truck struck him while he was changing a tire on the side of the road. Veronica had a dream about Jordan's father speaking directly to her, asking her to look after Jordan. Veronica knew Jordan was in a bad place, and she held his hand, both figuratively and literally, as he struggled to work through his grief.

Veronica generally looked after his well-being in every way possible. Jordan and Veronica decided that it would be fun to go on a cruise together, and they enthusiastically booked a trip to the Bahamas.

One week before they were to leave, Veronica called Jordan, and a woman answered. Veronica asked to speak to Jordan, and the woman sounded annoyed. When Jordan came to the phone, Veronica casually asked who the woman was, and he admitted it was a woman he had begun dating. Veronica was taken back a bit by this revelation, as she had thought they were exclusive.

Pushing back her surprise and hurt, she asked Jordan if their trip to the Bahamas was still going to happen. Jordan responded with an enthusiastic, "Yes!"

On the day before they were to board their ship, Veronica checked into their hotel room in Miami, and Jordan was not there. She left a note in their hotel room, in case he was running late, flagged down a cab, and went sightseeing for about three hours.

When she arrived back at the room and saw that Jordan was still not there, she tried calling him but could not reach him. Her intuition kicked in, and she knew that he was not coming. When she closed her eyes, she had a mental image of him lying in bed with another woman. They were kissing passionately, and when the phone rang, Jordan got out of bed, unplugged the phone from the wall, and told his lover, "She will never bother us again."

She left the hotel and walked a few blocks downtown until she found a hotel with a bar that looked inviting. Trying to shake her visions of Jordan, Veronica ordered a tropical-sounding drink, then another, and noticed that a man across the bar was smiling at her. She smiled back, and the tall stranger walked over to the bar and introduced himself as Peter.

They chatted for a few moments, she shared her story about Jordan, and when she asked casually what had brought him to Miami, he said he was traveling with four of his friends who were interested in a gang bang.

This shocked her, as Peter seemed particularly affable, and the term *gang bang* had a horrifically violent connotation. When she mentioned this, Peter assured her they were all nice, single guys trying to experience a fantasy and that neither force nor violence was part of their collective agenda.

Veronica said she was intrigued and went to their hotel room to meet them, partially because she was pissed at Jordan and partially because she noted ample security in the bar. When they got off the elevator at Peter's floor and she spotted another security guard at a kiosk, she knew she had an escape route should she need one.

She met the other guys, had a drink with them and some casual conversation, and Peter pulled her to the side and said, "You are a really nice lady. Why don't you leave? I don't want you to be a part of this. I promise you nothing bad will happen to the woman who spends time here, but you are just too sweet. If you were not upset about Jordan, you would not be here. You are like a sister, so just go now, before any of these guys become too interested."

Peter handed her a fifty-dollar bill. "For your next drink and the cab fare back to your hotel," he said and walked her to the elevator.

Once she arrived in the lobby, Veronica breathed a sigh of relief, thinking that the situation with Jordan was unfortunate, but she was glad she did not do something she would have later regretted.

She hailed a cab, and the driver, a young Hispanic man named Narlos, turned out to be extremely nice, funny, and a grieving widower.

Veronica questioned his unusual name, saying, "I have heard of Carlos, but not Narlos."

He responded in a wry and deadpan manner, "You, dear lady, assume that everyone can spell."

He turned to wink at her, and a feeling of generosity overcame her. Veronica asked him if he wanted to go to the Bahamas with her as a friend and said that the ticket was already purchased. "But," she added, "before you respond, you need to know there are three conditions. First, you cannot at any time hit on me. Second, we need a room change. We will have separate rooms. Third, you cannot at any time hit on me."

Narlos responded that she might have enjoyed too many margaritas because she mentioned the first condition twice, to which Veronica responded, "Nope, that condition is so important it needs to be repeated."

Narlos agreed to her generous offer and her conditions, and they set a time to meet at the dock the following afternoon.

They boarded the large cruise ship, and within an hour, Narlos tried to kiss her. Veronica promptly stomped on his foot with her high-heel shoe, causing him to wail in pain.

"Let me see your other foot. The condition was mentioned twice, and you violated it, so the punishment should be delivered twice." She was kidding. She smiled at him, he smiled back, and the two knew they had an agreement.

They enjoyed their time on the cruise and had some fabulous meals in the Bahamas. They were on the beach one day and met a man who was taking care of a yacht. He invited them to go deep-sea fishing. Later that evening, they made a bonfire near a secluded area of the beach where the yacht driver lived. They grilled the fish they had caught, along with some baked potatoes, and had plenty of sangria to wash it all down.

Unfortunately, Veronica had an allergic reaction to the seafood; she took two bites and felt her tongue begin to swell. Narlos got her some

Benadryl and looked after her. Veronica would regard Narlos as another one of her earth angels.

Jordan called her, completely unexpectedly, several months later, and apologized for his bad behavior.

"I wish I had gone on that cruise; I wish I had never let you go. It is and will remain one of my biggest life mistakes."

Jordan asked if they could start over again. Veronica said it was too late, that their moment had passed.

S&M , My Friend?

Not all of Veronica's relationships were hot and heavy romances. A few men came into her life with whom she enjoyed casual relationships or interesting friendships.

Asher was a bona fide, real life Indian prince. He was handsome, charming, and a total gentleman in every sense of the word. He did have one fetish. Asher was really into S&M. Like really into S&M. Veronica did not share his interest, but she did go to some interesting bars with him. It was kind of fun, like taking a walk on the wild side, but with a safety net.

And the people-watching aspect was incredible. Besides, Asher was nice, fun, wild, and witty, so she truly enjoyed his company.

Once, unexpectedly, Asher showed up at dawn at Veronica's apartment, completely beaten up. He had hooked up with an S&M girl who apparently was also really into S&M too. Judging by Asher's appearance, the girl got into her fetish very enthusiastically.

Veronica took care of his scrapes and cuts and gave him ice for his bruises. Asher still maintained that he had an awesome evening with the girl that Veronica nicknamed Maleficent.

Asher's parents had planned a trip to Africa and invited her to go with them, all expenses paid; all she was required to bring, according to Asher's mother, was her lovely self.

Their travel plans included a trip to Cape Town, Kenya, and Madagascar, which sounded amazing to Veronica. However, she did not go because work would not give her one month off. It sounded like the adventure of a lifetime, but *que será, será*.

Swinging from the Chandelier

Veronica met a handsome and charming man named Don in the banking world; they became casual friends and hung out at the popular and trendy Merc Bar, near her apartment. They never took their friendship to a level that included sex, although Don did try to make his moves! They became regulars there and became friendly with the bartender, James. In addition to mixing up some of the strongest adult libations in the city, James was a great conversationalist and a very chivalrous man.

He would keep an eye out for Veronica to make sure some of the more aggressive, less chivalrous men did not violate her personal safety zone.

While enjoying cocktails and conversation on a busy evening at Merc, Veronica felt dizzy, faint, and a bit nauseous, and wondered if she had consumed too much alcohol on a less than full stomach or if someone had slipped her a roofie.

Noticing that she looked a little out of it when she walked up to the bar to say good night, James offered to call her a cab.

"No thanks," Veronica said. "Think I've just been burning the candle at both ends. I'm going to walk home. It's not far, and the fresh air may revive me."

"You got it, gorgeous," James said, and he quickly scanned the bar shelves, picked up a business card, and wrote something on the back of it. He handed the card to Veronica and said, "Call me as soon as you get home. This is the phone number for VIPs only. The phone is here, behind the bar. Kind of a secret thing, you know. So, mum's the word..."

"My lips are sealed. I know nothing, and I speak nothing. Thank you," Veronica said and kissed James on the cheek.

When she had made her way to the door, she turned around and saw that James was watching her. She blew him a kiss, saw him wink back, and began the short trek home.

When she got home, she was barely able to close the door before passing out on the floor. She woke up sixteen hours later and thought, *Definitely a roofie.*

Savoring her morning coffee and a cinnamon roll, Veronica contemplated on some experiences in New York that had enriched her life. Some people brought grace and love to her life—true earth angels—while others refueled her distrust and increased her shield from the dark souls who tried to bring her down. Her hope was that she somehow enriched the lives of those she met as well.

Always an Empath

For most of her life, Veronica had been an empath. Her feelings were usually spot-on, and it could often be eerie and uncomfortable for her.

Veronica trusted her intuition. There were numerous instances when she was aware of health concerns and family dramas before they were made public.

Veronica knew her sister Mia was planning to divorce her husband before Mia had a chance to share the news. Veronica actually mentioned it to Mia the same morning Mia and her husband had made the decision.

She had a good friend, Michelle, in Dallas, and during a friendly phone conversation, Veronica encouraged her to revise her original plan to make the spare bedroom an office, and instead turn it into a nursery because she was pregnant. Michelle assured her she was not, but weeks later, she called Veronica and shared the news of her pregnancy. It was, of course, not news to Veronica, as she knew about it before the expectant mom knew. Veronica even correctly predicted the sex of Michelle's little bundle of joy.

There were a few occasions when Veronica's premonitions saved lives. Sitting at a bar in New York after a particularly long day at SIF, Veronica noticed the bartender seemed sad and preoccupied.

"You look worried," she said to the young woman.

"Yes," she replied, "I am worried about my mom. She just doesn't seem to be feeling like herself."

"You should encourage her to go to the doctor; I think her breast cancer has returned," Veronica stated.

The stunned look on the bartender's face at that moment was startling, but the look of gratitude when Veronica stopped in a few months later with a coworker for a glass of wine was especially poignant.

"I don't know if you remember," the bartender spoke softly, "but you told me that my mother's cancer had returned. I encouraged her to go to the doctor, and it had in fact returned. We caught it early, though, and the doctor said that made all the difference in her treatment and prognosis. I think she is going to be just fine. I am so happy that of all the bars you could have chosen that day, you picked this one. Thank you."

Veronica had a friend, Shauna, in Galveston, who had a boyfriend named John. When Veronica hung out with them, she could not help feeling that John had a black aura that surrounded him. She could not shake the feeling. It caused tension in her relationship with Shauna, who told Veronica she needed to try to be nice to him.

During coffee one morning, Shauna told Veronica, "You never talk to John; you stand as far away from him as possible. It's rude; it hurts his feelings... Please, can you stop?"

The last thing Veronica wanted to do was hurt her friend. She explained that she felt a black aura around John, and she really thought he was dying. Shauna thought Veronica was being ridiculous and stormed out of the diner. A few weeks later, Shauna called and said that a visit to the doctor revealed that John had lymph node cancer, and that the early diagnosis, along with a plan for aggressive treatment, would almost certainly save his life.

Storm Coming

One of the most poignant premonitions that Veronica experienced was the feeling that she needed to buy snow boots in late August. She became literally obsessed with buying weatherproof boots. It was on her mind night and day.

Her friends assumed that the blizzard that she had encountered during her first few days in New York City had freaked her out so much that her fear became irrational. They were also quick to remind her that there were in fact seasons in New York, and that they were currently trying to get through a heat wave and stifling humidity.

Still Veronica persisted with the need for weatherproof boots and bought a pair for herself and a coworker. She knew the coworker was just starting out in the city and really did not have any discretionary funds.

Two weeks later, one of the grayest days in American history happened, September 11. The city sidewalks at and around Ground Zero were covered with thick layers of ash. It was not the snowy blizzard that Veronica Mitchell had predicted, but heavy ashes from the remnants of what were once the twin towers. As unexpected as a blizzard in early September would have been, this was a nightmare of grave proportion—except waking up did not make it end.

Veronica witnessed both planes crash into the World Trade Center firsthand, and she bore witness to the unspeakable tragedy in the aftermath.

Chapter 4

Never Forget

On September 11, 2001, Veronica had traveled by bus to Hoboken to see clients. The trip offered a view of the Hudson River, framed by the vibrant New York City skyline that Veronica had seen countless times. And, the twin towers, those symbols of opportunity and prosperity, were always as compelling and powerful as the first time she saw them.

Veronica and her fellow passengers saw the first plane hit, then the second, and the bus driver received a radio dispatch directing him to stop and initiate emergency deboarding. The images of the twin towers, those formidable fortresses, on fire were forever seared into Veronica's memory.

In the sad days after the attack, Veronica saw on television that the Red Cross was setting up food distribution centers, and she and a few friends connected with officials near Ground Zero and began assisting in sandwich preparation for distribution to the first responders.

Joining countless other volunteers, Veronica handed out sandwiches to NYC police officers and firefighters. These first responders were tough as nails, dedicated public servants, yet many of them teared up when Veronica handed them sandwiches. For these reluctant heroes, it was surreal that amid the carnage there were people who would take the time to see that they were fed.

Some asked, "For me?" and made eye contact that conveyed feelings of sadness and despair. But there were also glimmers of hope and humanity, no matter how small, as they accepted the offering of food and the warmth of a hug.

This touched Veronica to her soul. The terror of that day would never be forgotten, but Veronica experienced firsthand that the best way to counteract unspeakable violence was with unconditional kindness. She made a promise to herself to support first responders as often as she could. Veronica would continue to organize fundraisers for community firefighters and help keep the spotlight on all first responders.

Bad Eggs

Though Veronica loved her life in the big city, there was no way to deny that living in Manhattan was expensive. Veronica knew of friends and acquaintances who had donated their eggs as a hope for infertile couples. In addition to helping people make their dreams of having their own little bundles of joy become a reality, donating eggs to a reputable fertility clinic paid very well. Veronica believed $10,000 for her donation to a worthy cause was not anything to dismiss.

When she went to New Conceptions Fertility Clinic for her initial consultation and screening, she struck up a conversation with a couple in the waiting room. They were expecting twins and were at the center for a routine checkup.

"Thank you for doing this," the prospective mom in the waiting room said when she found out Veronica's plans to be an egg donor. "People like you, angels like you, make this possible for couples like us. Thank you, because you change lives by helping to make parenthood a reality."

The woman had tears of gratitude in her eyes, and Veronica teared up as well. "You are welcome," Veronica eventually said. "I feel like I have had angels in my life too."

Veronica signed on to become a donor, completed all the testing that was required, and was moving forward with the program, which included painful daily shots. About four weeks into the process, she arrived home from a long day at work and noticed she had a message from the New Conceptions Fertility Clinic.

"Ms. Mitchell, this is Susan from New Conceptions." After clearing her throat a few times, she continued. "An additional review of your medical records indicates that your eggs are not viable to donate. It is doubtful that you will ever be able to conceive. Please stop by our clinic at your earliest convenience and pick up a check for five hundred dollars as compensation for your participation in the preliminary phase of our donor program."

Veronica replayed the message several times, as she was having trouble fully processing it. Understanding the message itself was easy but making sense out of her emotions was a completely different matter. Veronica had entered into the agreement with New Conceptions for primarily financial reasons. However, it had given her a sense of joy that she could be helping someone who otherwise would not be able to have a child.

But what about me? Veronica thought. *Did I... do I want a family of my own? Do I want to be a mother?*

Veronica was not sure. What terrified her was the thought that fate had closed the door on a part of her future without her having a say in the matter.

Be a Lion

Veronica Mitchell did have control over her destiny when it came to her professional life. She had an innate sense of design and creativity as well as a strong command of all things business related. She was also a compelling speaker with a commanding presence.

Throughout her career, numerous colleagues had asked her advice on public speaking and pitching ideas during meetings and presentations. In more cases than not, the queries came from women who often felt they had a hard time making their voices heard.

One woman asked Veronica during a group lunch how she was able to speak with such eloquence and ease. Her advice was simple yet profound: "Hold the room. Be the lion. Speak confidently when you have something to say. Do not simply talk for the sake of talking. People will begin to realize that when you do speak, it is important and relevant. Everyone will want to hear what you have to say."

Veronica noticed that her words had become mantras for some. She would see them posted on file cabinets and bulletin boards when she walked among the cubicles. Once she saw a Post-it Note on the mirror of the women's restroom. Beside the note was a stick figure drawing with the words, "I am a lion," encased in a cloud thought. It was drawn in red lipstick, and the simplicity of the drawing did not undermine its impact. It was on the morning of a staff meeting at Bellissimo Sei, undoubtedly left behind by an anxious colleague.

Veronica was never sure who left the note and drawing, but she did notice that during a major marketing meeting that a few junior level account representatives whom she had never heard speak had questions and comments during the meeting.

Never one to bask in her own glory, this made Veronica smile. She never felt threatened when women around her found the power of their own voices and achieved their own successes. She knew that many women seemed to fall prey to jealousy of other women, particularly successful women. Veronica hoped for a world where success and recognition were realized by as many women as possible. She wanted to be an agent of empowerment.

Veronica found it sadly ironic that she had such a supportive attitude for women in business, yet genuine, like-minded female friends were hard for her to find.

Rising Together

Veronica had a friend named Gerald she had first met during her early days in the fashion industry. He was the owner of a company called Millmoda that manufactured prêt-à-porter (ready-to-wear) clothing and intimate apparel. His company was losing money, and as he was aware of Veronica's keen business savvy, he did not think twice before enlisting her help.

"I want to hire you; I need to hire you. I feel as though I am hanging by a thread here, and the thread is thickening and becoming a rope that is going to strangle me. I am losing money... Please, can you help me?"

Despite his decreasing revenue, Gerald offered Veronica an attractive salary, and he was a friend, so there was no way she could or would refuse him. Plus, there were few things quite as intoxicating to the talented Ms. Mitchell as a challenge. She was in...

Game on.

One of her first entries in the success column was landing the largest retailer in the industry as a client. She managed the relationship with them very well; she tended to it like a well-nurtured rose garden. The company's executive staff promptly noticed her diligence and top-notch communication style. Each season they trusted her so much they allowed Veronica to write their purchase orders completely—an unusual practice by mega-million-dollar businesses.

Veronica knew that in the fashion industry an integral part of success was maintaining a diligent awareness of your competitors' offerings. She always had her competitors scoped out, knowing the products every company in her industry marketed.

She identified a bra she liked in Italy that had sold like gangbusters. In conjunction with her mega retail client, Veronica managed to develop a private label knockoff between the bra vendor in Italy, Millmoda in New York City, South Korea, and the retailer's corporate offices in Ohio for three years. The venture resulted in a substantial profit for all parties. Additionally, Veronica earned the distinction of being the only person in the history of the retailer allowed to do a private label for them outside of the company.

As hard as Veronica worked, she played and loved with equal gusto. Another dashing gentleman who shared the landscape of Veronica Mitchell's life was a former banking executive named Garit. He was twenty years older, and he had begun his pursuit of Veronica when she too was in the banking world.

Garit was a European man who opened Veronica's eyes to the extra dimension of joy that culture can bring. Garit spoke five languages, and some of his multilingual skills rubbed off on Veronica. She was able to speak some French, Spanish, Italian, and Arabic.

Garit had amassed quite the fortune during his days in the finance industry. He was a generous man who enjoyed lavishing his fortune on Veronica, buying her beautiful clothes and exquisite jewelry.

They spent their evenings dining in some of the trendiest eating establishments. They also enjoyed Broadway plays, cigar jazz bars, and art exhibits and genuinely enjoyed each other's company.

Garit and Veronica each worked near the Empire State Building, and they loved to go to a French steak house where a destined-to-be-famous chef worked. They used to eat there weekly. Veronica would ask for her steak to be prepared butterflied, which annoyed the hell out of the chef because he thought it ruined the flavor of the meat. He took every opportunity to playfully tell her that.

Veronica shared an enjoyable conversation with the soon-to-be-famous chef one night. They each stepped outside to have a cigarette as he spoke about writing his first book. He later gave an autographed published copy to her as a gift.

Garit and Veronica dated for eight years. They were great friends and had great sex, and they had great plans, dreams, and goals. Unfortunately, they were not shared goals.

Garit was divorced and had two children and was not interested in marriage or having more children. By this time, Veronica was in her early thirties, and she wanted to have kids. She had made a conscious decision to ignore the egg donor reports from the in vitro clinic. Their opposite desires created an undesired tension between the two.

Free to Be

Most people in the fashion world were women or homosexual men. Veronica met a gay man named Andy, and they became close friends instantly. Andy was a men's underwear rep, and they used to travel together for trade shows. They enjoyed hanging out at bars and speculating about the straight or gay factor of every man that walked into the particular bar they were at that evening.

They would order their drinks from the bartender, along with an appetizer or two, and then catch up on the day's news or intriguing gossip or ponder some of life's deep questions. When they began to feel lightly toasted as Andy used to say, he would move in closer to Veronica and say in his best game show announcer voice, "It's time for another edition of 'Is He Straight or Gay?'"

Andy would put extra emphasis on the word *gay*, drawing it out for effect. It was hilarious; and a few times it caught Veronica off guard, causing a mouthful of wine or beer to spray all over the bartender or table because she simply could not contain her laughter.

Veronica and Andy really were great friends; they had such an easy rapport when they were together. Once they were walking home after an evening at one of the city's finest bars, and Andy commented to her that most people fear the gay world. He explained, "When I talk about aspects of my lifestyle to some of my family or friends, they get freaked out. Then they become judgmental, but you don't. I've always felt that you like me for me, that you could give a rat's ass about my sexuality."

The truth was... Andy was right. She loved him for who he was, and who he was spectacular! Veronica also prided herself on being open-minded. She always believed people should be free to be who they were... sexually, spiritually, and creatively.

She found it easy to be that way living in New York City since it was so diverse and had such a collective spirit of openness and acceptance. Veronica had lived between Gramercy Park and Little India. She had also called both the Upper West Side and Upper East Side home. Each place possessed its own set of cultures, people, and mind-sets. She felt that living in New York had helped shape the person she had become, and she genuinely liked that person.

Veronica had also met many European men during her time in New York and her numerous travels to Paris. She found European men to be exquisite! They were dashing, charming, romantic, and chivalrous, and they tended to treat women as if they were royalty.

Of course, as every princess will tell you, the world is not made up of only princes...

There are some toads and some creeps.

Onward and Forward

Veronica knew from seeing the devastation of September Eleventh first-hand that life can end in a second. She felt the need to make some changes, to be true to herself, to get, as her good friend Andy said, "goddamn real."

Veronica broke up with Garit, as she knew the relationship had been coasting along on borrowed time for too long. Garit did not take the breakup well. He called her every day for a year offering her marriage and a baby. He sent dozens of red roses often. Veronica had to say no to his proposal each time he offered.

The truth was it was simply too late. She loved him dearly, but their romantic chapter had ended. Veronica had moved on. Their friendship however did not.

Veronica would always regard Garit as a gentleman and best friend. She wanted nothing but the best for him, and she knew he felt the same way about her. She hoped they would be friends for life.

Veronica made another big decision. She moved from New York City to Galveston to take marine biology classes at Texas A&M.

Game on, Andy, she thought. *I am getting goddamn real.*

Chapter 5

Seas the Day

Veronica Mitchell took a long look at herself in the full-length mirror on her closet door. The little girl with blonde curls and rosy cheeks did not stare back; in her place was a stunning young woman. She still had blonde hair. It was full and wavy, and it was one of Veronica's best features—a Leo's mane. Her hazel eyes were still beautiful and engaging, and she had somehow managed to retain her creamy, porcelain complexion.

She was slender, but not too skinny. Her male friends described her as thin, with curves in all the right places. She did find time to work out, and it was obvious. She was both beautiful and cute. She was a tomboy and a sensuous woman.

After the attacks on September 11, Veronica engaged in more than just an assessment of her looks. She spent considerable time on self-reflection. *How should I spend my life? What else have I always wanted to do?* Her life had been incredibly successful, but she could not shake the feeling that it could be more fulfilling, more authentic to her true spirit. Life was short and precious, and she realized that it could end at any time without warning.

One of her dreams had been to become a fashion executive, and she had dazzled companies in the fashion industry with her talent and business savvy. Veronica had built a reputation as a highly competent professional who knew how to get things done with flair and finesse. She had also transformed a friend's financially troubled company into a thriving one that realized almost immediate profits of over $1 million.

Considerable accomplishments aside, Veronica Mitchell was a woman with many layers, and she knew there were still many to peel back. She loved animals and remembered times in her life when a cherished pet was like a best friend to her. And the ocean had always gripped her with a magical, almost metaphysical hold.

She cherished her childhood memories of the Jersey shore. In adulthood, every cruise she took was as breathtaking as the first. And all ocean creatures truly fascinated her. Never one to procrastinate once she had a plan of action, Veronica moved to Galveston, Texas, and enrolled in the marine biology program at Texas A&M. She kept her job at Millmoda in New York City, but she delegated some of her responsibilities to her protégé Nick.

This was the best of two worlds for Veronica—she could pursue a lifelong passion, and she could fly to New York City, Los Angeles, Chicago, Dallas, Boston, Barcelona, Las Vegas, Paris, or wherever she was needed to tend to work-related issues. As always, she just made it all work. Life made simple by Veronica Mitchell.

Absolutely in love with her new course of study, Veronica absorbed her professor's lectures, soaking up every word. She felt invigorated and enjoyed the feeling of pursing another passion.

Student life included her volunteer work with a marine biology rescue lab. She fell head over heels in love with a baby dolphin named Cory. He was rescued after he was injured by a fishing line and separated from his pack.

Veronica befriended a woman named Jenna, who was the head of the rescue lab department, and they spent countless hours playing with Cory in the pool.

Cory was as playful as a young puppy. However, he was three hundred pounds of sheer muscle, and bruising was a natural consequence of being his playmate. The baby dolphin did not intend to cause harm; he just loved playing with his favorite humans. Some of Veronica's happiest moments were those spent playing with Cory. Aside from the sheer joy the young dolphin derived from all this attention, it also helped prepare him for his future as one of the stars of a therapeutic recreation program in the Florida Keys for children with autism.

A Tornado Within

College was a breeze for Veronica this time around, just like before. *People actually have to study for tests*, she often thought. She absorbed every drop of information. Her favorite professor named Trevor, who infused his lectures with energy and passion, capturing her completely. She respected his knowledge and teaching style. He respected her ardent love of learning and her ability to retain vast amounts of information. She was his only student that made 100 percent on every test.

Similar in age, Trevor became a trusted friend and introduced her to colleagues who were professors at the University of Florida. They extended her an offer to visit, and she gratefully accepted, recognizing it for the immense honor it was. The tour of their marine mammal labs was fascinating, and she relished seeing the current projects they were working on.

At the end of the visit, the professors insisted on taking Veronica to dinner. Veronica was blissfully in her element as they discussed ways to optimize the relationship between marine biology and business. *I'm a lucky girl*, she thought. *I always seem to have opportunities to be with like-minded people, and it's fantastic.*

Veronica also became involved with another organization focused on saving manatees. It was a wonderful collaborative venture; she provided pro bono merchandising and marketing advice for them. In return, the famous organization donated some signed items for Veronica's favorite charities.

Her life felt full and complete. So far, she had discovered few downsides to life in Galveston.

An exception was certainly that living in Galveston brought with it the possibility of frequent hurricanes, and Texas was also located in the middle of Tornado Alley.

On one occasion, Veronica had to fly to Fort Lauderdale for an important marketing meeting with a Fortune 500 client. She did so with full knowledge that a hurricane was predicted to strike Galveston then Florida.

Mother Nature kept her word, and the hurricane announced its arrival early. Veronica drove forty-five minutes to the meeting, dressed in her business best, in torrential rain, with high winds and tree branches hitting her windshield. It was terrifying, especially since she was alone.

Radio reception was sketchy at best, so she tried to keep her fear at bay by thinking of all the songs she knew that had the word *wind* in the title.

"Blowin' in the Wind." Yikes, reaching back, she thought, chuckling anxiously to herself, *"Run Like the Wind." "Wind beneath My Wings."*

"Oh, I almost forgot," she said aloud. "'*Candle in the Wind.*'"

She began to sing loudly, hoping her voice would mask the sound of what was now hail hitting her windshield.

"Never knowing who to cling to when the rain set in."

When she thought about the song's words, she realized the lyrics were not optimal for her peace of mind, and instead she focused on her talking points for the day's meeting.

She arrived safely at the hotel, put away her belongings, and reviewed her notes for the meeting. The meeting was successful, although briefer than had been originally planned due to heightened fears about the hurricane's increasing strength.

That evening, Veronica took a nice long bubble bath and sipped some white wine she had purchased in the room's minibar. Later that night, the hotel lost power, as did their backup generator. Luckily, she had bought a flashlight from the hotel's gift shop earlier in the day just in case, along with a New York Times best-selling book, and read by flashlight until she dozed off.

Power did not return until later the next day, and the aftermath of sand and ocean-water-flooded streets delayed her departure home by a few days.

During another business trip, she was driving along a scenic back road from Fort Worth to Dallas. Out of the right of her windshield, she noticed a large tornado, approximately a football field length away from her, churning its way across the open fields.

Veronica noticed there were no nearby homes, cars, ditches, or anything remotely resembling part of a viable exit strategy or safety plan. This was a time before the advent of today's cell phones so all she could do was keep driving alongside the tornado. It was her constant companion for about fifteen minutes before it dissipated. She wanted to stop and regain her composure but kept going for fear the formidable funnel would resurrect itself and make her its target.

She drove another twenty miles and then stopped at a corner general store. Knowing she had no business activities scheduled for the remainder of the day, she searched the store for a bottle of wine to enjoy in her hotel room. All she could find was a bottle of red grape wine with a redneck name that boasted an alcohol content of 18 percent.

That will work, she thought as she grabbed a bag of extra spicy nacho chips to accompany her hotel room happy hour.

She slept through most of the night but woke up at 3:30 a.m. feeling parched, as if she had consumed an entire bottle of tequila, downed a shaker full of salt, and then licked several limes. She got out of bed, grabbed the bottle of hillbilly heaven to pour the rest of it out, and noticed the bottle was empty. "Well, fuck me, that explains a lot," she said, surprised at how raspy her voice sounded.

The trip back to her Galveston home after her meeting was uneventful with no weather events. Later that evening at home, one of her friends called and invited her to a tequila and taco party. Veronica thanked him but declined the invitation.

During her time living in Galveston, she had to evacuate her beach house in Galveston twice, but luckily, her home incurred no damage either time. The ocean waters just flowed under the fifteen-foot stilts.

Travel Time, Anyone?

While she loved the marine biology program and living in Galveston, she had become quite accustomed to travel. Her career, the men she had become involved with, and her extended and varied circle of friends had opened her eyes to the endless enjoyment of exploring new cities and cultures. Travel was an integral part of her life.

One holiday season, while her family was away for Christmas, Veronica decided to book a cruise to Belize. Cruise ships left regularly from the port of Galveston, and the fact that she would be traveling alone did not deter her. She had never had a problem finding adventure when she traveled solo.

On the first day of the cruise, she met a couple, Mary and Dave, and their son Jacob. Jacob was handsome and charming but happened to be five or six years younger than Veronica. She could not help but think of him as the younger brother she never had.

The family essentially adopted her, and the foursome had a fabulous time together. They went swimming with nurse sharks and stingrays, feeling like they were the stars in an underwater adventure movie.

They went dancing and gambling, and they enjoyed fabulous meals and cocktails with exotic names. This was the ultimate getaway for Veronica—the ocean, marine life, food, drinks, dancing, and great people who became her surrogate traveling family.

On a subsequent trip, accompanied by friends from Texas A&M to Costa Rica, she visited the Costa Rican Marine Mammal Program. In meeting the right people there, she found out the entire program fell under the leadership of the Costa Rican government, and their hope was to advance the program.

Veronica's education and extensive business experience completely wowed the VIPs of the program. They were convinced she was the woman they needed to achieve their goal of expanding their program. They offered her a position that sounded like she would have considerable professional autonomy. Her responsibilities would include writing a strategic business and marketing plan along with supervising its implementation. The job required that she live in Costa Rica for a period of three years.

About two weeks prior to starting the position, her always-right clairvoyant gut, told her not to take the job. Veronica listened to it and declined the position. Working for a third world country government was just too much of a risk.

Emotionally Killed by a Mercenary

Confident she had made the right decision; Veronica was content to return to her life and her studies in Galveston. In one of her classes, she met a man named Derek. He sat in front of her and took advantage of every opportunity to turn around, catch a glimpse of her, and strike up a conversation.

Derek was a military firefighter and a private security contractor, more commonly known as a mercenary. He was very tall, dark-haired, and striking in a mysterious sort of way. Veronica noted that the first time he turned to speak to her his smile looked like one he had perfected while staring in a mirror. She imagined him standing there until he got every angle right. The smile was charming but perfunctory.

The two of them had a first date, which lead to a second, then third, and before long they were in a relationship. They had exciting sex, heightened by what always seemed to be an ever-present aura of danger.

Their sexual relationship never became physically threatening, but there were times when the intensity pushed beyond thresholds Veronica had ever experienced. There was a sense of being outside her own body, of not knowing where Derek's physical presence stopped and hers began.

The physical sensations reminded her of past pleasures she had experienced, but they were tinged with the excitement of unknowns she had not.

When they were out in public, Derek would tell people he was a firefighter, and after accepting well-deserved praise and thanks for his service to the community, he would tell them, "I love helping my fellow man, and my long-range plan is to become a doctor. Veronica totally supports my dream. As a matter of fact, she has offered to pay for medical school."

The first time Veronica heard those words, and knew he truly meant it, she realized he saw her as his sugar mamma. He winked at her and added, "Isn't that right, babe?"

She had always had an affinity for the word *babe*. It was such a loving and personal term of endearment. Sweet, sensual, intimate... "Love you, babe," or "Need anything, babe?" or "You look amazing, babe."

When Derek used the word, he smiled that same smile he always smiled every single time. A flash of perfect white teeth, his upper lip with a quick, slight quiver, akin to Elvis. The brown eyes focused on his subject, engaged them, then the mouth closed, the eyes seemed to retract, and his expression faded to neutral. She hated to think it, but it was almost reptilian. It was icy and calculated. With an involuntary shudder, Veronica thought, *Mercenary man smile*.

When Derek invited Veronica to go to Maldives with him, she declined his offer. As much as she had always dreamed about spending time there, she was troubled by his increasing lack of commitment to her and their relationship. She knew he was seeing another woman behind her back. She also had growing concerns that Derek was demonstrating signs of becoming psychologically and emotionally abusive.

She noticed this after she had started a women's rugby team with her friends in Galveston to accompany the men's rugby team that most of her friends played in. Derek complained that he did not understand why she was hanging out with her bar guy friend, Miguel, and going to all the rugby games, playing medic.

"You are so busy and have so little free time. Don't you want to spend your free time with me?" he pleaded. He told Veronica he simply did not understand why she needed anyone else but him.

A legend in his own mind, Veronica thought. She saw his protests as an attempt to control her. Turning the tables on him, she told him he certainly seemed to need more than her companionship. "You are messing around with other girls, or at least one that I know of," she retorted to the six-feet, five-inch mercenary man. "If you are serious about me and this relationship, let's get serious. Otherwise, I am fine on my own, I have a full life, and I will not be alone, unless I want to be. If you are not in my life, Derek, I won't be devastated."

Shortly after that exchange, Derek was called to go to Kosovo for six months. He and Veronica spoke on the phone often, although the conversations felt more like mind games orchestrated by the mercenary man.

When he suddenly stopped making contact for several weeks, Veronica reached out to his commanding officer to make sure Derek was okay. Despite her concerns about the state of their relationship, she certainly did not wish him any ill will. That phone call completely pissed

Derek off and resulted in a huge fight. And, just like that, contact with the often-volatile man stopped in full.

Approximately eight months later, she received a call from Derek. He announced he was back in Galveston and wanted to see her. Veronica had essentially moved on with her life, and she was quite surprised to hear from him.

They went to dinner followed by sex, and Veronica knew that night that they had conceived a child. She could not explain how, but there were no doubts in her mind. She just knew. Despite the fact she was on birth control, she simply knew she got pregnant.

After six weeks, terrible morning sickness began, so Veronica took a pregnancy test and was not surprised with the positive result. She called Derek and asked to meet him at an Italian restaurant that had become one of their favorite places to dine. She wanted to tell him about the pregnancy in a public place, where there was less chance of him becoming volatile.

She broke the news to him calmly and told him she knew she could not raise a child alone. Her job required frequent travel, and from a financial perspective, she did not think she could afford it. Plus, she had been told her eggs were not viable, and she had no chance to carry to term.

Additionally, Veronica questioned Derek's fitness for parenthood, citing his issues with commitment, and the danger and unpredictability of his job. "I just don't think you are ready for the enormous responsibility of parenthood," she calmly stated.

Derek protested, saying, "We can find a way to make it work, somehow." She started to counter his assertion when he quickly added, "I never back down from a challenge. Ask anyone."

Angered that he was again only thinking of himself, she fired back quickly, "We are talking about a child, Derek. This is not a mission, and this doesn't require marksmanship or sniper tactics. The opinion of your comrades is not relevant. Having this baby is not in the best interest of anyone, first and foremost, this baby."

Derek's expression went blank; he seemed to look completely through her. She didn't listen to what he said, didn't pay attention to his words, but she got the message that he did not agree with her assessment of the situation, particularly his parental worthiness. She really didn't care at this point. Her mind was made up. The wisdom of the clearly more competent potential parent was going to prevail. Derek offered no additional argument. He gave her the money for an abortion and left.

The next day she suffered a very painful miscarriage alone. The physical pain and nonstop hemorrhaging lasted about three days, but the emotional pain was much harder to endure.

Veronica was overwhelmed by sorrow—from past to current abuse—to the loss of her child.

If only circumstances were different, a baby with the right man... If only I could carry to term.

It was too much. She was worn out, depressed, and so very tired deep in her soul.

So, Veronica mindfully paid all her bills for three months and organized paperwork to ease the handling of all by others then downed a full bottle of aspirin and dined on lobster, crab, and calamari.

Knowing anaphylaxis would set in, she put on her best pajamas and snuggled into bed. All went dark. Then all was vividly bright.

A brilliantly shining figure literally carried her out of bed into her bathroom and forced her to throw up. She felt him by her side, coaxing her body to remove the toxins.

The phone rang as she lay there on the floor, in shock and in awe.

"Hey, beautiful, it's Miguel. I miss you and need you. When can I see you next?" he asked into her answering machine. His voice was like an angel calling her back to life.

After her body felt healed, she and Derek slowly began to spend time together again. When they had sex, it was very rough and angry. Caresses were not tender. What were once softly spoken words had become raw and provocative. He did not hurt her, but it felt like a game of domination and control. It was a dance with love-hate choreography.

Veronica interpreted it as anger over her saying she did not want a child with him. One evening she went to his house and discovered that he was not alone. There was a girl there, so Veronica broke off the relationship. It was a decision she felt confident in. It was a decision she knew she had waited too long to make. She was no one's fool or sugar mamma, but had been his too long... *why?* She shamefully could not answer her own question.

Veronica knew she would always remember Derek. The feelings she associated with him were not warm or sentimental. Her time with him had been tumultuous, filled with his emotional and psychological games, plus roughly attempted control. She knew she would never forget the pregnancy and the miscarriage. She was less certain about how those experiences would affect her later.

Next-Level Vibrating

Sometimes soul mates are not lovers that become life partners. Maybe the timing isn't right, or two people are in different places in their lives, or geography, or prior commitments throw huge wrenches into the equation. Sometimes there just cannot be a traditional fairy-tale ending. Miguel taught Veronica that.

She had first seen Miguel in Cádiz, Spain, when she had spotted him at the table next to hers during lunch and they had locked eyes. Then again on a big screen at a Garth Brooks concert in New York City.

Later she found out he was a student at Texas A&M, and they knew many of the same people. Uncanny. Fate. Destiny.

They officially met in Galveston at a bar called Shot Absorbers that was a favorite hangout for most A&M students, including Veronica and her friends. Again, they locked eyes, but this time it was for the entire night.

Over time, they enjoyed casual and flirtatious conversations at the bar, and eventually Miguel asked her out.

On the evening of their first date, Veronica waited forty minutes for him to show up before calling his home. A friend answered, and Veronica could hear his conversation with Miguel.

"Oh, man, I totally forgot. Can you ask her to come over? I am so not ready for *her*."

"No can-do, man," the friend said. "Your date, your deal."

Veronica heard the muffled sound of the receiver falling, and Miguel retrieving it midair. "So sorry, sweetheart," he said, sounding perfectly charming, and Veronica suspected, perfectly stoned. "So much has been going on. I completely forgot about our date. I could never forget you, but I did forget about our plans," he continued. "But, hey, why don't you come over here? A bunch of us are hanging out. It'll be fun."

Veronica paused for a moment before responding. She was angry. This was supposed to be their first date, and as much as she genuinely liked Miguel, she was not in the mood to accept rude behavior. *Nope*, Veronica thought.

"Wow, you forget our date, and your idea of making it up to me is having me drive to you. You sure know how to make a girl feel special." Her tone was calm and relaxed, but she wanted him to know she was not pleased. "Thanks, but no thanks. I don't necessarily expect to be wined and dined, but I would like to be more than an afterthought." She paused before adding, "See you around."

Despite being born into an affluent family, Miguel worked as a bouncer at Shot Absorbers, the bar Veronica and her friends visited weekly. They ended up chatting a few times and agreed to try another date.

"This will be a great second date, Veronica," Miguel said. "Any special requests?"

Veronica winked and said, "Yes, don't forget!"

Their date began with a casual and tasty dinner and then a stop by another A&M bar. Eventually they were joined by some of his friends. One was a girl named Bethany who gave Miguel an enthusiastic hug and became his shadow for the duration of the night. A shadow that parked herself in his lap literally. Veronica was pissed that Miguel did not encourage her to get her ass up and find alternate seating and that he allowed her to be a part of their date at all.

Veronica told Miguel that she was leaving; his actions were unacceptable for a date. She called herself a cab and went home. She was not mad; her telepathic intuition told her that they would continue to run into each other, talk, and have many interesting and beautiful hookups.

Every time after sex with Miguel, Veronica's whole body vibrated. It felt so strange and never happened before or with anyone else, only Miguel—every time. Even when he would just walk into a place where she was, Veronica vibrated. They would continue to be there for each other as the years passed.

Miguel was not destined to be a love interest, but rather a great friend. The passage of time proved it was clear they were soul mates. He became her confidante, guarding all the secrets of her heart, and she wanted the absolute best for him. Their relationship would truly stand the test of time. She loved him. He loved her. For life. Uncanny. Fate. Destiny.

Taken Woman

Zander was another man in Veronica's life in Galveston who lived by what she came to refer to from experience as the dick principle—a combination of mind games, unreliability, and selfishness. Almost every female friend of Veronica's knew at least one man for whom this seemed to be a guiding principle, so she wondered if there was a manual these guys read.

"Excuse me, Tom. Can I borrow your dick manual?"

"Sorry, I loaned it to Charlie, and he loaned it to some other prick."

Zander was a man she had begun dating after she and Derek ended. She would see Zander at Shot Absorbers, and she always noticed that he stared at her. She literally caught him staring constantly, intently—like "does he ever blink?" stares—every night she was there.

One night after liquid courage in the form of tequila shots, she walked up to him, wedged herself between his bar stool and the occupied bar stool beside him, and asked, "Why do you always stare at me?"

She expected some form of an embarrassed apology. Instead he replied, "Because I am in awe of you."

Completely caught off guard by his straightforward response, she simply said, "Okay, thank you, bye, see ya," and returned to her seat.

A few weeks later, Zander invited her to a party at his condo. When they had a few moments alone, he told her, with the same unapologetic candor, that he wanted to be her man. Veronica mused that there was something to be said about a man who knew what he wanted. So, they began dating.

It was a good relationship when they were alone. Sex with him was erotic, sweet, gentle, and loving. Their texts and calls were romantic and special, complete with intimate pet names and tender couple speak.

However, when they were out in public, Zander avoided her. It was maddening to Veronica, and after numerous and frustrating conversations in bed, he finally admitted that he knew Veronica was a taken woman. Apparently, Miguel had put the word out that she was his.

"Zander, you do realize I am a grown woman, independent, capable, self-supporting? I am not property that individuals can lay claim to... You do get that, right?" Although she thought in her mind, *Miguel does have me.*

The exchange that followed was humorous to Veronica as Zander was deadpan and straight-faced when he told her, "Word on the street is 'hands off Veronica,' and believe me, Miguel has eyes everywhere."

One night while snuggling in bed together, Zander and Veronica talked about their individual lives and future. Veronica had to go back to New York City because their biggest client was demanding she be there for a few years to run another multimillion-dollar project, and they would only partner with Millmoda if she ran it.

Veronica made the decision that she was not going to continue with school. She had received all the accreditations she needed to continue with both the mammal rescues, which she had grown to love so much, as well as conducting necropsies. And she was so grateful for the opportunity to have met so many people in the program, people she now called friends.

That night, Zander proposed to her, but Veronica declined. She knew it was his last effort to keep her there and that he was not truly ready to marry her. A future together just wasn't in the cards for them.

Self-Destructive Vices

Another enduring relationship in Veronica's life was her relationship with Robbie. He became an indelible part of the landscape of her life. A beautiful man with a beautiful soul, Robbie was a very generous friend to Veronica.

Robbie had attended Southern Methodist University, and he and Veronica had literally run into each other on and off for thirteen years, first meeting in downtown Dallas. They had partied together and enjoyed casual hookups throughout the years.

Transitioning out of the mind-set of an ever-partying student was a change that Robbie was not able to make. He continued to drink to excess, and many of his phone calls to Veronica started out with, "I got so wasted last night," or "Tonight we are going to get totally blitzed."

Veronica knew Robbie was an alcoholic, and she had noticed that he could not last an hour without a drink. He would drink, be the life of the party, get belligerent, get the shakes, and then drink again. The cycle repeated itself. Drink, drank, and drunk.

After a weeklong New York City visit by Robbie, he asked her to move to Dallas with him. He had a large, beautiful house, and he felt it could only be a home if she lived there too—if she would be his life partner.

"I could live with you; we could build a life together. I can do the whole settle down, put down some roots thing with you. I can do that, Robbie, but I cannot do the partner/wife of an alcoholic. It is hard, exhausting, and I can't watch you do that do yourself. I will not be part of that. Please check into rehab. If you can do that, perhaps we can build that life together."

Robbie agreed and checked into rehab as soon as he returned to Dallas. Veronica breathed a sigh of relief and was hopeful for the future, but then he called her three days after he started rehab and said, "Wow, I am so drunk."

"I take it you checked out of rehab," Veronica said solemnly. "A perpetual college student," she said softly to herself.

"I tried, Veronica. I tried to do what they said, but they are all so different and desperate. They are not like me, and I am not like them. I am not an alcoholic."

About ten years later, Robbie sold his large Dallas home and moved in with his parents. He called Veronica to let her know. She hoped that his parents would see his alcoholism and try to stop him from damaging himself. She knew in her heart that if he were not an alcoholic, they still could have a life together as man and wife.

Robbie taught her that love on the run did not always have to mean stolen trysts in between career demands. It was not always fated to be random hookups from city to city. Nor was it limited to relationships that were meaningful but short-lived pursuits.

Sometimes love arrived with packed bags, dropped in for a visit, and then departed with a kiss. However, the departure was always temporary, and love always returned, picking up exactly where it had left off.

But Veronica Mitchell was an incredibly smart, very creative, and insightful woman. She was also extremely compassionate and never made important life decisions without listening to her almost-psychic intuition.

She poured her heart into her friendships and relationships, sometimes giving more than she should and sacrificing her own feelings. She listened to her gut and knew when to call it quits, when to say goodbye before she allowed her heart to get trampled on. She worked hard and loved hard, and quite honestly, Veronica would not have it any other way. Her soul would simply not allow her to do so. Thus, the hope of a life with Robbie ended.

Chapter 6

Wild Hearts Cry Too

The fact was that being back in the Big Apple again seemed perfectly natural to Veronica. She identified herself as a New Yorker. She had lived in New York City on and off for fifteen years now and had spent most of her formative years in New Jersey.

She loved the culture; she loved the diversity; and she loved that she could order groceries, food, or pretty much anything else desired in the city and have it delivered. She could even order pot and did so when Miguel came to visit. Most importantly, New York City was unequivocally the best stage for her keen business prowess and her precisely honed set of skills.

Veronica did not simply get things done in the business world. She was a force to be reckoned with. She was not afraid to dig at the core of a problem—elbow-deep in viscera—and analyze it objectively before determining the best course of action. She was a fixer.

Veronica felt that this attitude toward problem solving was a vital key to her success. It had helped her become a first-class business executive at age twenty-five, managing fashion lines in various cities in the United States, then extending her prowess to cities in other countries.

She had radically altered a company's culture. She had repositioned brands. She developed new product strategies. She had tackled large problems faced by companies that would otherwise snowball, spiraling out of control, threatening the very life of the business.

Veronica knew that in the business world, there was not a chance to slow down, take a break. There was a pulse to every business, no matter how shallow, and there was a heartbeat, no matter how faint. The blood needed to keep coursing, and better strategies needed to be implemented while day-to-day operations continued. Often Veronica felt like she was changing tires on a car that was still running.

Each time Veronica celebrated a business success, she tipped her hat off to her dad, who had instilled in her a tough business sense. Inside, she winked at her mom for teaching her a woman's strength... *Hear me roar, Mom!*

She did encounter personal setbacks and heartbreaks, but the business world kept her distracted and happy. Yes, she was molested, raped, her heart played with as if she were a toy doll by various men, and so much more, but business saved her.

Veronica Mitchell became numb to the heartbreak, an internal, unrelenting sense of fear and lack of trust. She stopped shedding tears and simply stood, walled sky-high and bulletproof... or so she thought.

Bienvenido Miami

Shortly after her return to New York City, Veronica and her assistant had to fly to Miami for a swimwear show. It was an important trip. Veronica was planning to meet her swimwear vendor in Miami, who was flying in from Italy.

There were numerous flight cancellations and delays on the day of the show. Veronica was a VIP flyer, so even though most flights were canceled, her frequented airline was able to secure a flight for her group.

She was plagued by a sense that something was off. Veronica's psychic signals were firing on all cylinders. She could not define it clearly. She just felt a heavy sense of uneasiness. Had the trip not held such high importance, she would have been tempted to cancel her travel plans.

Living as an empath had taught her that she needed to pay attention to the messages, the chatter, and the images that came to her. LaGuardia was one of the busiest airports in the world, so finding a quiet place to meditate was an impossibility.

Veronica found a small, reasonably quiet area near the seating at one of the gates. She decided she would sketch—it always provided her a chance to express what was going on in her mind. Often, sketching helped her release thoughts and feelings she would not otherwise be able to articulate.

She pulled her sketchpad out of her briefcase, along with her pencils, and began drawing whatever came to mind. When she was finished, Veronica glanced at her drawing. There were flowers, butterflies, a profile of a random stranger's face, and thickening billows of dark clouds that seemed to jump off the paper. Veronica stared at the clouds, waiting for some possible message. None came.

When they arrived in Miami, she and her assistant boarded the elevator to their hotel room. Veronica had a huge and heavy trunk full of trade-show items. When the elevator doors opened, Veronica tried to push the trunk out of the elevator, but the floor was uneven and the trunk fell back on her, twisting her body and her knee. Veronica's kneecap was literally displaced to the backside of her knee.

After enlisting the help of guests coming out of their rooms, Veronica was able to exit the elevator and pop her kneecap back into place, before falling to the floor in silent pain while she awaited the arrival of an ambulance. *Dark, billowy clouds*, she thought.

The first responders included a handsome EMT who was very diligent but had a bedside manner that seemed to include extreme flirtation. In between monitoring her vital signs, he hit on Veronica the entire ride to the hospital. He asked for her phone number, saying that he made it a point to follow up with patients he transported.

Against her initial better judgment, she did give him her phone number. He called her every day, and he even came to the trade show one day to ask her out. Feeling that he was just a bit too pushy and perhaps a bit too weird—who hits on a woman who just broke her knee? —Veronica told him she was not interested.

For the remainder of the trade show, Veronica worked from a wheel-chair. She could not walk and had no choice but to find a way to work through the pain.

After considerably more hardship, deliberation, and pain, Veronica's protégé Nick arranged to have another assistant, Sookie, fly down to help Veronica in Miami.

Initially, Sookie was a godsend—she helped Veronica secure an attorney who later won a judgment of $25,000 from the hotel in Miami for the uneven elevator floor that caused her injury. She even moved Veronica to a five-star hotel that was more spacious, as well as wheelchair-friendly.

Sookie began going out each day for breakfast, lunch, and dinner and frequently meeting friends in the evenings at bars. Veronica continued to work, in a diminished capacity and in increasing pain, and her two assistants appeared to be enjoying a dream vacation at the expense of Veronica and their company.

Help Me Home

After the swimwear show in Miami was over, Veronica was still in tremendous pain. She flew back to New York City to see an orthopedic physician, who sent her to physical therapy for six months. His treatment plan for her was continued physical therapy, sans corrective surgery.

An ongoing battle ensued between her physical therapist and her orthopedic physician to determine whether she needed to continue physical therapy or undergo surgery.

All Veronica knew was that she was in pain, she was not getting any better, and she desperately needed help. The only temporary relief she found was during her weekly visits to an acupuncturist by her apartment who had studied across Asia and India. A great bond was made between them. He saw how much she was suffering and did all he could to ease her pain. To her surprise on her final visit, he got on his knees and presented her with a precious gift, a sacred cloth given to him by the Dalai Lama, something Veronica would always cherish. He was there for her when others refused, in her time of need, bestowing unbelievable gifts upon her— pain relief and his sacred cloth.

Veronica had contacted both of her best girlfriends, but they were far away and embroiled in their individual lifestyles full of unfaithful and ungrateful personal dramas. They refused to help Veronica even though she had been a good friend to each of them.

She even called Miguel. He was currently dating an attorney who was very jealous of his friendship with Veronica, so Miguel feared he would harm his relationship with the lady lawyer if he came to assist Veronica.

Thank goodness for her ex-lover Garit and protégé Nick. Otherwise she would not have survived the daily life on her own. Some would say that living in New York City as a single woman was tough enough. Trying to navigate in her injured state made it damn near impossible at times.

One time she actually was stuck in her bathroom tub for three hours... she had accidentally fallen in while at her sink. Her New York City apartment bathroom was tiny, and she simply could not maneuver her way out.

The gift of hindsight provided Veronica with a bittersweet perspective when she thought of those painful days. It had been hard, lonely at times, and frequently challenging. However, she again proved to herself that she had the grit, grace, and perseverance to make it through whatever life threw at her.

Big Hurdles, Little Rocks

Veronica's road back to recovery was tumultuous. As if it was not hard enough to be a strong business warrior, while wielding crutches and dealing with knee pain, she had to deal with insurance drama. Her health insurance would not allow her to see another physician in New York City for some complicated reason, but did allow it in Little Rock, Arkansas, which was, at this point, near where her parents had retired. Veronica meditated on her situation. She was after all a problem solver, a fixer, and there was no challenge too big for her.

After sitting uncomfortably on her fire escape to watch the Macy's Fourth of July fireworks display, cocktail in hand, she cried. *Enough is enough.*

Veronica shifted into total badass mode and applied those formidable skills as a fixer to her own current situation. She made the decision to rent an apartment in Little Rock, so she could see a physician who would immediately perform surgery on her knee. He had studied her X-rays, reviewed her treatment history, and had been forthright in informing her that surgery would not completely resolve all her knee issues, as the extended physical therapy had damaged her knee cartilage. There was the chance that she could face a lifelong battle with arthritis. Veronica understood that the pain could be chronic and may at times affect her mobility, but she knew it would never stop her indomitable spirit.

But before she left the Big Apple, Veronica had a one-night stand with a handsome billionaire named Brayden, introduced to her by her bartending friend. Perhaps it was the chronic pain, or perhaps the bittersweet feelings associated with leaving New York City again, but whatever the reason for her last big city fling, Veronica had no idea at the time that she would soon view him as one of her angels on earth. It would become apparent that Veronica met him at exactly the right time.

In addition to being insanely wealthy and handsome, he was also very well connected and influential. Veronica's New York orthopedic physician had appalled Brayden with his unprofessionalism, seeming indifference, and lack of responsiveness. Brayden surprised her by successfully getting the doctor's medical license revoked at his expense. Chivalry was alive, well, and living in New York City! What a man, what a mighty fine man!

It did not take Veronica long to be settled in her new life in Little Rock. She was able to fulfill the duties of her New York City job with a tiny puppy on her lap (a poodle she adopted to encourage her healing and to make her walk three flights of stairs several times a day). She knew her job inside and out, and backward and forward, so working remotely was not a problem, and it allowed her parents to help her navigate through her days.

She met many nice neighbors in her apartment complex—a woman named Jaimie, a man named Glen, and an elderly woman named Claudine helped her when needed. Since all of them had adorable puppies, they shared cocktails overlooking the sunset almost every week.

Veronica enjoyed the positive, healing environment of her new, albeit temporary, life in Little Rock. She was surrounded by great friends, lived near her parents, and still was able to do the work she loved, in the city she loved, just from a distance.

A Natural Born Businesswoman

One of the major reasons Veronica was so successful was that she had wanted to be part of the business world most of her life. While other young girls dreamed of weddings, picturesque suburban houses with rose gardens framed by white picket fences, and babies, Veronica Mitchell dreamed of seeing different cities, countries, and cultures through the eyes of a successful businesswoman. She envisioned conducting staff meetings seated at the head of a long table, asking every person for their ideas and contributions.

It was not as if she felt she had to prove anything to anyone, nor was it that her self-worth was tied to how successful she was. It was simply who she was. She knew she was born to manage, born to lead. Her father had instilled in her the knowledge that she could be successful, and that was her greatest source of inspiration and power.

Living Realms

Veronica Mitchell's life was comprised of more than her professional and personal worlds. Another realm of her existence—the in between world of her experiences as a clairvoyant empath—defined her as equally as any business strategy she had successfully implemented or any relationship she had formed.

For most of her life, Veronica had been able to see people's auras as clearly as she could see their clothing. There were times when she would meet a person and immediately and innately attach a feeling to that individual. This happened frequently with people she sensed to be toxic.

At other times she could be in a crowded room, and the chatter of strangers' thoughts, assumptions, and perceptions would be completely deafening and emotionally draining.

Her dreams were often extraordinarily vivid. As in the past with her concerns of her father's health, her dreams could be eerily identical and occur in successive nights. The emotions and feelings associated with her dreams were powerful, and unlike the dreams that most people had that were easily forgotten upon awakening, Veronica could remember hers in striking detail.

Chapter 7

Healing Hands

Although Veronica would always cherish her memories of living in Galveston, and in many ways, New York City had felt like home, healing in the slower paced environment of Little Rock was exactly where she needed to be now.

Veronica was a good person with a kind heart. Her personal credo was that being a good friend meant that you were there when someone needed someone to listen and when they needed a shoulder to lean on. But when Veronica needed that sympathetic ear or comforting shoulder, her girlfriends had been unwilling to reciprocate.

Historically, the joys of having a great gal pal or two had eluded Veronica, but she was young, alive, beautiful, and healthy aside from the chronic and very frustrating knee pain. She was living in Little Rock and was able to fulfill the duties of her job in New York City remotely, still traveling as needed.

She had met some nice neighbors, and there seemed to be the possibility that some genuine friendships could develop with these women. And she had the support of her parents who were less than an hour's drive away.

Veronica embraced her life as it was now, and her mantra was an Italian phrase she had learned from a coworker at Bellissimo Sei: "*Non è mai troppo tardi per ricominciare.*" Or as her English-speaking colleagues would say, "It's never too late to start again."

Supermodel Tease

Veronica's business acumen remained spot-on regardless of where she called home. She had brought in a Spanish men's underwear line run by the dynamic team of Javier and Isabella.

Javier's best friend was a supermodel named Carlo. Veronica had the pleasure of meeting him, and her first impression was that he was a freaking Adonis. Simply put, he was drop-dead gorgeous. In life, when things seem to be too good to be true, they typically are.

In Carlo's case, his too-good-to-be-true turned out to be that he was only available to a certain half of the population. Carlo was gay, much to the dismay of heterosexual women and to the delight of gay men.

Carlo wanted to have a baby, which did not necessarily mean he wanted to be a dad. His life was full, and he was adored and in demand as a supermodel. He enjoyed the kind of wealth that carried privilege. His life was not limited to black and white. It was a kaleidoscope of color that extended way beyond margins.

Veronica had the opportunity to spend time with him through her business relationship with Javier and Isabella.

One evening, over dinner in New York City, Veronica and Carlo each talked about their desire to have a child.

After each of them honestly assessed their current relationship status, they agreed the only way to make that happen would be to draft a baby contract.

Veronica was very happy about the chance to have a baby, and she was excited to talk to Miguel about the contract. They had made plans to meet in Central Park later that evening. They were going to share a bottle of champagne and toast each other and their enduring friendship.

Miguel and Veronica hugged when they saw each other. They held hands, they danced even though there was no music, and they saw only each other even though the park was brimming with visitors.

Veronica told Miguel about the baby contract she was considering, and when he paused for a few moments, she was smiling, inside and out, waiting to hear him protest that the two of them would have their family, no contract involved.

Then he told her she should go for it, and Veronica swore that the cracking, then crumbling sound she heard was her own heart breaking.

She tried to process the words Miguel had spoken but was distracted by the physical sensation of a sour warmth rising from her stomach. The sensation stopped just before it reached her throat, and she could neither speak, nor exhale.

She was not sure what was going to happen next. What in the world was going to happen next? Would this be the end of their story? Would this spot in Central Park, on this day, at this hour be their last moment as Miguel and Veronica? They had discussed having a family together; they both felt it was their destiny. Veronica wanted her fucking destiny.

Veronica felt a huge pang of uncertainty and feared that the feeling would last.

Miguel looked at her tenderly and said, "We have always had a connection, and we always will. We are soul mates, no matter who else may enter the picture. I'm involved with someone now, just as you have been involved with other men. Veronica, our relationship has never been simple or been defined by preconceived standards of... hell, I can't explain it. We are just a constant in each other's lives. Complicated, yes. A sure thing, yes. There you go—we are a fucking complicated sure thing."

Carlo had a lawyer on retainer who drafted a contract for Veronica and him. During the forty-eight-hour consideration period prior to signing, Veronica could not shake her intuitive early warning system nudging her, then kicking her, to let her know that the arrangement would not work.

Certainly, Carlo was gorgeous, worldly. He spoke ten languages, was a gentleman... He was not just another pretty face. However, he was undeniably a diva, and Veronica feared that she would end up being the main caregiver and financial provider, so she backed out of the contract.

Meanwhile, the American division of the men's fashion line was doing well under Veronica's leadership. Javier reported this good news to Veronica during a conference call. He shared that the Spanish division was not doing as well as he had hoped. Javier voiced that he also aspired to launch an Asian division of the luxury underwear line.

Veronica was not only blessed with a powerful telepathic component of her being, but her business sense enabled her to read between the lines and predict how conversations would play out. As Veronica sipped her coffee and picked off pieces of her bagel, she waited for the proposition that she was certain was coming.

Javier asked Veronica to move to Barcelona to get the Spanish division back on track, continue to run the mega successful American division, and launch the desired Asian division.

Javier explained that the move would come with a large salary, a paid and furnished apartment, and a personal expense account. He gave her a robust twelve hours to consider the offer.

The reality was that there really was no consideration period needed. It was her job, and Javier was a major contract, her contract that she had brought in. If she did not accept, there could be negative implications to her career. Veronica did not want to take the chance that her reputation as one of the brightest and best fixers in the fashion industry could be damaged.

Veronica packed her bags and prepared for international life. It was both exciting and terrifying. She struggled with fears that she may never put down roots. She had concerns about her on-again off-again relationship with Miguel, as well as anxiety about leaving a burgeoning support system.

She acknowledged her fears and drew upon strength from an inner reservoir of serenity, acceptance, and faith. She was first and foremost a warrior, and in typical warrior fashion, she forged ahead.

$$Chapter\ 8$$

Bon Día, Barcelona

Javier and Isabella did not secure an apartment or a visa for Veronica as they had promised. They put her up in a hotel suite for two months, but not for an uninterrupted two-month period. Veronica would have to check in and check out as needed to accommodate guests who had long-standing reservations. She quipped to Isabella that at times she felt like a bag lady schlepping her luggage back and forth.

"But, darling, you have such stylish bags," Isabella responded in a playful voice.

Veronica's life was moving full steam ahead, powered by sheer force and determination. She was unstoppable. She simultaneously managed the flourishing American division of men's apparel, maintained oversight of the growing Asian division, and resolved the issues plaguing the Spanish division.

A typical day for Veronica began at 6:00 a.m. She would go with Isabella to the gym, and then they would drive to the quaint little fishing town of Montgat, where the office was located. Her day at the office would end at 9:00 p.m., but she would work at home until midnight in order to manage the American team.

She had always been exhilarated by challenges and looming deadlines. As a fixer, she created the promise of possibilities where none had previously existed. However, she had begun to feel a little less invigorated as the days continued to be especially long and grueling. She felt as if she was singlehandedly running the Spanish company and all its divisions out of her suitcase.

Among the distractions that Veronica enjoyed—when there were opportunities for downtime—was the culturally diverse dining at exclusive restaurants with Javier and Isabella. She also traveled to Amsterdam with Isabella where a favorite pastime of the two women was smoking hash. Lots of hash.

And they went to Croatia where they rented a car and drove through Vidova Gora, which boasted the highest peak on all the Adriatic islands. They sunbathed in Korčula and walked the beautiful historical areas of Dubrovnik. Veronica marveled at the beauty of the vast and picturesque country.

She enjoyed the occasional evening out with her coworkers Adalfo and Felipe. They would go barhopping and casually stroll street fairs or find live music. She appreciated the chance to unwind without her bosses being present.

One particular evening Veronica went salsa dancing with her new Spanish tribe, and she was toppled by a man who could barely stand, yet alone dance. It was obvious the partygoer had downed more than his fair share of tequila.

She was certain her arm was broken, and her coworkers rushed her to the closest emergency room. The trauma room staff wanted all of Veronica's companions to clear the ER, but she wanted at least one to remain, as she did not speak Catalan well. Veronica was allergic to NSAIDs and aspirin and needed someone who spoke the native tongue to make sure the doctors and nurses knew that.

Still, a communication breakdown occurred, and the ER nurse gave her aspirin, but luckily Veronica did not have an allergic reaction. She figured the volume of alcohol in her system prevented any ill effects.

Although the attending physician did not diagnose her arm as broken, an American physician later confirmed her suspicion.

Those who viewed Veronica's life from a distance may have been envious of the allure and glamour of travel to exotic locales and mingling with fashion executives, artists, and celebrities. She earned a high salary, and Javier and Isabella covered her personal expenses, but she felt a loneliness that cut deep to her soul.

She missed her dog Marley, whom she had given to her sister and brother-in-law, Tuni, to care for while she was in Barcelona. Marley was not merely her pet. He was her best friend.

She longed for Miguel's presence deeply. His absence created a void in her life. She woke up thinking about him, and he was the last thing she thought about when her head hit the pillow at night.

During one of their phone conversations, Miguel told Veronica that he very much wanted to visit her in Barcelona, and she was giddy with joy as she anticipated his visit. She squeezed in time for a manicure and pedicure and bought a sexy new nightgown. She even managed to carve out a few chunks of time to spend with Miguel.

Three days before he was to arrive, Veronica had a dream that Miguel met a woman who intrigued him. The dream was so vivid it startled her out of sleep. Less than five minutes later, she received a text from Miguel: "Love you to the moon and back, but something has happened. I met a woman, and I am feeling like I want to see if this goes anywhere. I will need to postpone my visit. I know you understand. Love you, sweetheart."

Veronica put her phone on the nightstand and pulled the covers over her head. She could not say she was surprised at Miguel's text, as she had just dreamed the scenario. She would have preferred that he cancel his visit because of a reason not related to affairs of the heart, specifically his heart, as he pondered an affair with a possible new love interest.

As for Veronica's own heart, it ached with a familiar pain, and she said softly, "My heart hurts." It hurt just as it had in elementary school when she was bait for bullies. She wished she could visit Ms. Beth and the school nurse for some sympathy, juice, and animal crackers. She wanted her mom. She felt sad and alone. She cried until sleep eventually cradled her in its arms again.

Veronica felt frustrated that Javier and Isabella had not followed through on both conditions they had proposed as part of her moving to Barcelona. Eventually, they did put her up in an apartment that they owned, but they never got her a work visa.

That meant that every five weeks Veronica had to leave Barcelona, and Javier and Isabella had to pay for her travel to another country. She visited Holland, France, and Croatia, and before going on a planned trip to Sicily, Veronica decided that she was done. *No más. Terminada.*

Veronica was tough. She could persevere, but being a fixer meant you had to know when things were tired, broken, or in need of a recharge. At this point in her life, she was all three.

She was heartbroken about Miguel and tired of living in a place where she felt limited control over her life. Veronica also worried about Marley and hoped he was receiving the quality of care he deserved from her brother-in-law.

He had continued to ask Veronica for additional money for Marley's care, citing that the brand of food they bought was on recall or that they needed to find a new vet because their favorite had relocated. Before she knew it, Veronica ended up paying over $1,000 a month for Marley's care.

Tuni provided pictures of Marley, and she could see that he was indeed receiving loving care. Veronica was grateful to be able to put her mind at ease about the situation. She simply did not have any energy left to devote to more worry or stress in any area of her life.

Acknowledging that her life was seriously out of balance, she made the decision to move back to New Jersey temporarily, with the longer-range plan of relocating to Florida.

There were important matters she needed to tend to that required her presence in New York for the American division of the men's line and New Jersey to tie up some legal matters, and she had to pick up Marley.

She appreciated the opportunity to further experience the European way of life and culture that living in Barcelona had afforded her. In many ways, it had been the opportunity of a lifetime. But not at the expense of her well-being.

Veronica could honestly say she was leaving Barcelona with a clear conscience as all divisions of the men's apparel line were doing well. As Javier had said on many occasions, the company was *pateando traseros serios*—kicking serious butt.

She knew she would be able to carry out her responsibilities with Javier from New Jersey. She carefully considered all aspects of moving back to the States and felt that all systems were go. Veronica was optimistic about the new life she was trying to carve out for herself.

As for Javier and Isabella, they were less than thrilled with the turn of events. They wanted Veronica to remain in Barcelona long term, but they also knew she was essential to the continued success of the men's line. If she needed to perform her duties long distance in order to continue her business relationship with them, they had no choice but to comply.

The move back to New Jersey was uneventful, even routine. Veronica was used to moving from city to city, state to state, and country to country. She could contemplate a major move with a relative ease that most people could not even comprehend. In her world, picking up and moving without the luxury of prolonged planning was a common occurrence.

She rented a small apartment and furnished it with the possessions that were the most comforting and sentimental to her. All items that were too large or did not blend with her much-needed calm and chill mind-set went to storage.

Veronica also enjoyed a wonderful reunion with Amanda, a childhood friend from New Jersey she had not seen in many years. As a single mother, Amanda had certainly experienced her own struggles with financial and relationship drama.

She had worked and studied hard to advance her career; she had entered the medical field as an LPN and was now a nurse practitioner. She was able to provide a good living and happy home for her daughter, as well as derive personal satisfaction from her work. She had also formed friendships with other moms in her neighborhood. From Veronica's observation, Amanda had indeed done very well.

Veronica was successful in getting her legal issues wrapped up with little difficulty or disruption. She had her sweet dog Marley back; she had spent quality time with both Mia and Amanda. She was ready to implement the next step in her plan, a move to Tampa.

Veronica was happy to have her dad help her with her move from New Jersey to Tampa. This would be their second cross-country trip, and it would prove to be one of Veronica's most memorable. He had accompanied her on her first trip to New York City, the trip that literally marked the beginning of her career.

Now she was a success in the business world, inspired in great part by the man seated in the passenger side of her car. Mr. Mitchell randomly pushed buttons on the radio, and they played "name that tune." They commented on the scenery around them—abandoned farms with rusted tractors and out of commission grain elevators. They drove by vacant country stores and corner shops with nailed plywood sheets where windows once were.

Within a few miles, they passed sprawling neighborhoods with impeccable landscaping and billboards boasting the availability of spacious new homes, priced from $600,000 and beyond.

They passed through a small town nestled near a bayou with low-hanging cypress trees and a sign that read, "Moorsland, Population 652." There was a family diner, Katie's Kitchen, which was in a state of collapse as the wood from the second story had decayed and fallen into the first floor. Near the diner was a once viable real estate office with a window sign that had originally read, "If you lived here, you would be home now." The sign, vandalized with spray paint, now read, "If you live here you have been forgotten."

Veronica pulled into the parking lot adjacent to the diner and the real estate office. "What happens to people who live like this? Are they just forgotten?" she asked her dad.

Proud that his daughter had not lost her sense of idealism and was a good person with a good heart, David Mitchell replied, "You don't forget. You do the best you can to be the best person you can. All your successes with the companies you have worked for, you made them bigger, more successful, so that they could hire more people. Maybe not people from Moorsland, but maybe from towns like this one. The work you did with all the marine animals in Galveston—someday, a child will gaze with wonder at those dolphins and feel infinite possibility. And that dolphin you worked with, Cory, he went on to help kids with autism in a therapeutic recreation program."

Veronica felt tears well up in her eyes as her dad continued.

"You are proving every day that little girls can grow to be women who can do anything they put their minds to. I came from humble beginnings, and I worked hard to be successful, and I have two daughters that followed my example. That is my point... success is like a single lit match. When you drop it to the ground, it catches fire, it engulfs the areas around it, and unless you try to stop it, it can't be contained."

Veronica choked on her words as she spoke. "Dad, I just want to say—"

"You're welcome," her dad interrupted. "I am so very proud of you." He grabbed her hand, and they sat there silently. The moment was too beautiful and too poignant to mar with words.

When they arrived in Tampa, Veronica's dad helped her get her apartment set up. Her mom remained in Arkansas where her sister Mia had moved temporarily as she recovered from the emotional and financial blows of her divorce.

They had made plans for a Mitchell Family Christmas. Veronica's nephew Dustin was planning to fly down to Tampa for Christmas, and her mom and sister would drive down as well.

Veronica had shared with Amanda that she had moved to Tampa, and Amanda told her she would come for a visit.

Within minutes of Amanda's arrival in her apartment, unexpected drama ensued. Amanda had received a phone call that had upset her greatly, to the point where she was screaming obscenities and crying hysterically. Veronica tried to console her, but she pushed her away, called a taxi, and left with no explanation.

Veronica's dad listened but did not intervene as he felt that Veronica would be able to diffuse the situation. He was very concerned, as he had known Amanda as a teenager when she and Veronica spent lots of time together. Amanda spent many overnights at the Mitchell's home and was a regular guest for dinner. He also knew, from his wife's conversations with Amanda's mother, that their family life was not always stable. He was genuinely fond of Amanda and feared she was in a bad place.

In fact, David and Laura Mitchell had spoken several times since Amanda's arrival and sudden departure. They were each worried about her.

Amanda called Veronica the next morning and said she was staying in what she described as an upscale hotel, and she asked Veronica if she could come and get her.

"Of course," Veronica answered without hesitation, "but can you tell me what's going on? I have never seen you like this. Amanda, you looked, acted, and sounded so out of control—nothing like the woman I spent time with in New Jersey recently."

"Seriously, Veronica, you are interrogating me now? I am so sorry that my life did not end up as perfectly as yours."

Veronica glanced at her dad who overheard the conversation. In an instant, she could not help but notice that her dad did not look well. He seemed tired, and when she asked if he was okay, he said that he had been doing a lot of consulting work lately and that it had just taken its toll on him.

She remembered her dreams about her father's health when he was staying with her in her first apartment during her first trip to New York. The dreams were so real and so vivid, she would wake up paralyzed with fear.

Looking at him now, she could not help worrying that history was repeating itself. "Dad, it's not ulcers again, is it?"

He reassured her that it was not.

Veronica went to see Amanda as promised. Immediately upon her arrival, she asked Veronica for money to pay her hotel bill. Veronica refused because she did not understand why Amanda would check into a hotel she knew she could not afford.

"I can only assume that you knew you could call me and that I would pay your bill and take care of everything," Veronica said. She was deeply hurt that Amanda would take advantage of her.

"Screw you, Veronica. All you have ever done is abandon me."

Before she could react, Amanda struck her on her cheek. Veronica recoiled in pain not only from the blow, but also from the pain of seeing what had happened to her friend. Amanda and Veronica did not speak again for four years.

While living in Tampa, Veronica met Yvonne, a friendly woman who also had a dog. They took their dogs for walks together, and they became good friends. Julia, who had moved from Galveston to Washington DC, then to Tampa, was also a friend.

Veronica also had a friend from work at a Fortune 500 company named Scarlett, who did not like the way their bosses treated Veronica. Veronica was being sexually harassed in a "cannot report you" kind of way.

Veronica's friend Brayden, who was her last big city fling in New York, had an oceanfront mansion on Saint Pete Island, and he rounded out her entourage of friends quite nicely. Other than Yvonne, Amanda, Julia, and Scarlett, Veronica had not enjoyed strong friendships with women.

Veronica worked for a start-up fashion company that required her to travel to New York occasionally, which she loved. As she knew the fashion industry in New York like the back of her hand, she was an excellent consultant for them.

She had obtained her position at the company in an interesting manner. While she had been living in New Jersey, she had a phone interview with the owners of the company, Cassie and Kevin. They were very impressed with her, so they flew her to Miami for a face-to-face interview conducted on their yacht.

The start-up company's owner Cassie attended Florida Institute of Technology. She hired her boyfriend Kevin to help her run the company. Cassie's parents financed the entire brand with Veronica landing them amazing sponsors.

A famous artist from New York was part of the design team. He was so impressed with Veronica's business sense he asked her to work with him directly. His plan was his own apparel line based on his art. Veronica respectfully declined his offer.

Veronica parted ways with the fashion brand because Cassie and Kevin were assholes. They demonstrated this in every action, in every decision—literally every time either one of them would open their mouths to speak. They had a sense of entitlement beyond anything Veronica had ever seen.

True to character, when she informed them of her decision to leave, they tried to sue her. Her trusted lawyer in New York reassured her by phone, "The brats do not have a legal leg to stand on, literally or figuratively."

Not all the decisions Veronica made while living in Tampa were as easy as leaving the start-up company. As a successful businesswoman, she was used to making decisions that promoted success and built a foundation for future growth. Her decision to have a hysterectomy was a painful one that did neither. It felt like a door slammed on one of her lifelong dreams.

The surgery was medically necessary to correct health issues that had plagued her for years. Still, Veronica choked on the pain of knowing that she and Miguel would never be the family that she always thought they would.

Despite her hectic schedule and Miguel's carefree, partying lifestyle, she always thought there would be more time—time to slow down, time to embrace a life in which they were a couple, complete with children and the comfort and security that came with the knowledge that they were next to invincible together.

Miguel was not happy with her decision to have a hysterectomy. Upon hearing she had her surgery scheduled, he began sending her pictures of adorable babies. On one particularly adorable picture, Miguel had written, "I think this little guy taking his first steps looks like a Miguel Jr., don't you?"

Veronica explained to him her reasons behind needing the hysterectomy, and he understood, at least intellectually.

The night after her surgery while she lay recovering, Miguel got drunk and hooked up with a woman he had gone to high school with. When he told her this on the phone, she knew instantly that he had gotten her pregnant.

And in fact, Veronica found out about six weeks later that the woman had become pregnant. The family that she and Miguel had always hoped for would now be the family of Miguel and this random woman. To add insult to injury, Miguel told Veronica the woman would only keep the baby if they got married.

Veronica had planned to fly to Chicago to help him decide what to do, but he called to let her know he got engaged, so she canceled her trip.

Since the moment she and Miguel had locked eyes, he had been her rock, part of the life force that flowed through her body, the love of her life, confidant, and best friend. He would catch her when she fell, literally and figuratively. It was evident that they were not going to work romantically, but they worked beautifully in every other way.

There had been too many distractions caused by too many men and women that had coursed through their lives. They each had focused on business, and the rewards and pleasures that came with success. The sad reality is they fell prey to the myth that time would somehow stand still for them, allowing them the chance to become the real family they had always longed for—or at least that Veronica had.

Chapter 9

Fatal Attraction

Laura Mitchell sent her daughter a video showing the surgical removal of a part of her arm due to skin cancer. After viewing the video, Veronica immediately called her mother, primarily to see if she was okay, but also to find out why she had not previously shared either her health concerns or the surgery with her.

"Mom, did you hear the one about the daughter who lived in a far away land who received a video from her mother? She was so excited to see it because she needed a loving message from home."

"Veronica," her mother tried to interrupt.

But Veronica continued, "Instead, she saw a video of a surgery removing a part of her mother's arm. Mom, what the hell?"

"Well, honey," Laura Mitchell explained, "these things are just a part of life. You have been away from home for so long. I guess we just became accustomed to living our daily lives and doing what needs to be done."

Veronica suddenly felt a terrible twinge of isolation from her parents. When she tried to visualize the most recent image she had of her parents, memories of her mother and father during her childhood and teenage years began flooding through her mind. She could not conjure an image of them in later years other than an occasional holiday gathering, the moving trips with her dad, knee assistance in Little Rock, and the random business trips her mom joined in on.

Veronica thought maybe she needed to move closer to home. She felt that as important as her professional life was to her, she did not want to be a stranger to her parents. They had always been her greatest cheerleaders, and they were responsible for shaping her into the competent business-woman she was today.

She thought of one of her coworkers at Bellissimo Sei, a sweet woman named Connie, who had confided in Veronica that her mother had passed away without her really ever getting the chance to know her as a person.

Veronica knew that she did not want to be that daughter. She knew she left to start her career and begin her life before she really had the opportunity to know and see her parents through adult eyes.

"Veronica, are you still there? Did I lose you?" Her mother's voice sounded worried through the telephone receiver.

"I'm still here, Mom. You know I have been thinking lately that I could live closer to you and Dad, if there was a position available, maybe in Arkansas or Tennessee?"

"Well, honey, that would be great. I will certainly keep an eye out for something that might interest you. And I will ask my poker friend, Mary Alice, to ask her daughter to check for positions that may interest you."

"I didn't know you played poker, Mom." Veronica chuckled.

"Oh, honey, I am full of more surprises than a case of Cracker Jacks," Laura Mitchell said.

Veronica had traveled more times in her life than she could count for business. If she relocated closer to her parents, it would be the first time she had ever moved solely for personal reasons.

She really did not need to mull it over. It felt like the right thing to do. Now all she had to do was find a job.

"No big deal," Veronica said softly. "I got this."

Nepotism and Deceit

In her late thirties, Veronica was hired as the director of marketing at a community organization in Tennessee. She did not foresee any difficulties in promoting the gracious living to prospective residents. The community offered a beautiful and convenient way of life.

Shopping centers were located within walking distance of the homes. The manicured landscaping was lush and plentiful as trees and flowers were planted alongside most streets. There were hiking and biking trails for nature enthusiasts, as well as tennis, racquetball, and basketball courts for athletes of all skill levels. High-speed commuter rails made travel for workers in nearby urban centers effortless. There was even community-wide free Wi-Fi.

While working as the marketing director, Veronica was asked to sit on the board of the personnel hiring committee as they conducted interviews for a general manager. Using her significant business and financial expertise as a reference point, Veronica was not overly impressed with any of the candidates.

Taylor Davidson, an auto dealership manager who had a degree in accounting, seemed to be the preferred candidate among Veronica's peers.

"He is so inspiring," her colleague Nancy said.

Smooth talker, Veronica thought.

"He seems like he is very comfortable in a leadership role," another coworker chimed in.

A confident demagogue, Veronica mused silently.

There were a few comments about his decisiveness when he responded to the group's questions.

His way, or the highway, Veronica imagined writing with chalk on a large blackboard.

She had sized him up him as a snake oil salesman, which she voiced to board members and colleagues, but he seemed to have successfully wooed the deciding executives.

Taylor was hired, and on his first day, he called Veronica to his office where they shared coffee, large pastries, and small talk. The conversation eventually shifted to his vision for the community organization.

He told Veronica that he had done his homework on everyone in the company. He was impressed with her background and her experience, and he gleaned that she had a very strong business sense.

"Can I speak frankly?" he asked her.

"By all means," Veronica responded.

"I feel like you are overqualified for the position of director of marketing. Frankly, I can see you as the director of operations, or even chief executive officer, you know, at the helm."

Veronica was flattered and started to speak, but Taylor raised his hand, palm out, in a stop gesture, and continued. "The thing is, for that to happen for you, it needs to be the right environment, the right company, and this is neither."

He stood up, walked directly in front of Veronica, and leaned against the desk, then delivered more of what was surely a rehearsed speech. "This is my time; this is where I will succeed. I have worked too hard to allow myself to be compromised in an environment where there is a potential threat to my success. I am on the fast track, and as for my destination, let us just say the sky is the limit. I cannot and will not allow anyone to change my course of action, my destiny. I am charging full speed ahead; I am full throttle."

Veronica could tell that Taylor was trying to sound like Wall Street, but he was coming across like NASCAR.

"Work here if you must, collect your paycheck, pretend you are going to tap that pretty little head up against the glass ceiling, but you will never rise above me."

He paced a bit before he delivered his summation. "Play by my rules, don't disrespect me in front of anyone in this office. Try to throw me under the bus or stop me, and I'll make sure the first tire marks are on you."

Taylor glanced at his watch, and Veronica took the cue. "Thanks for the coffee and the chat, and in case I have not yet stated the obvious, welcome to the community."

As she walked toward the door, Taylor responded, "I gotta check some items off my to-do list before I attend a big welcome dinner event tonight. Have a good day."

Pig roast? Are you the guest of honor or the entrée? Veronica thought. *Will they put you on a spit and serve you with some roasted potatoes?*

Veronica turned around, flashed her best Joan Crawford "don't fuck with me, fellas" smile, and said, "I won't have it any other way."

Shortly after Taylor Davidson was hired as general manager, it was announced that the director of finance and founder of the community, Maggie Addison Rubinstein, would be walking away from her duties for approximately two years as she and her husband were adopting a baby. The company would be recruiting for an interim replacement.

Veronica was enmeshed in a comprehensive marketing campaign, so she was not upset when Taylor left her out of the interview committee. There was a sense of urgency, and within two weeks, the community organization welcomed Laverne De Luca as its interim director of finance.

Ms. De Luca had respectable business experience, having held accountant roles in two companies, as well as volunteer board management experience in a few nonprofits. Perhaps the most interesting aspect of her background was that she had known Taylor Davidson since they had attended the same high school for a few years and had been friends ever since. They had even worked at the same company, years after graduating from their respective colleges.

And here they were, working together again. Davidson admitted that he had spoken to De Luca about the opportunity but denied that any undue influence had been exerted that would favorably affect her hiring. There was no doubt that something shady was happening since the other candidate was a lot more qualified.

Three days later, Laverne De Luca's biography was disseminated throughout the company, as well as to the movers and shakers in the Tennessee city. Knowing the history between Davidson and De Luca, Veronica wondered if she would be a female version of toxic Taylor.

The following Monday morning meeting kicked off with De Luca's introduction to the group by the sabbatical-bound Maggie Addison Rubinstein. De Luca was petite, pretty, and polished. Veronica would have liked to call her assertive, as she admired strong women, but by the close of the meeting, Veronica observed that De Luca seemed to switch between an aggressive and passive-aggressive persona.

"I am so thrilled to have this opportunity to work with y'all," De Luca began.

Veronica immediately pegged her as fake and opportunistic.

Y'all? Veronica thought.

De Luca was born and spent her formative years in Boston. Her family moved to New Hampshire where she attended the same high school as Davidson for two years, and then she was accepted at a college in Vermont. Veronica bet a round of cosmopolitans that up until today's meeting, the word *y'all* had never crossed De Luca's lips.

The meeting went south quickly as De Luca informed the team of her need for total loyalty and devotion. And, of course, she gently reminded everyone that anyone in the room would be offered up as a sacrificial lamb before De Luca took the fall for anything that happened in the company.

The message was received loud and clear by all those De Luca referred to as *y'all*.

It did not take long for Veronica to see Taylor's shady dealings. He had deferred money from the company's marketing budget for personal gain, cut back on security costs so he could use the funds on self-promotion, overspent on a new real estate division with his family's contracting business benefiting, and much more.

Taylor would routinely call Veronica to his office and yell at her for a whole host of reasons, the majority of them pure bullshit. Taylor was clearly threatened by Veronica as she had business experience and an impressive résumé that boasted success with many well-known companies, both national and international. Taylor could not have possibly demonstrated more insecurity and fear about being upstaged by a woman than if he made it his full-time job.

Veronica let De Luca know some of Taylor's shady dealings, adding that she no longer wanted to report to Taylor. She told her that in addition to all his "personal gain" ways of conducting business, he verbally abused her regularly.

Veronica made sure that De Luca knew that Taylor was not the first asshole she had dealt with in her career. She just could not stand being berated by someone for whom she had so little respect.

Veronica went on record stating that she would never quit. They could either let her go or put her under someone else, so De Luca made the decision to have her report directly to her.

De Luca suggested to Veronica that the best approach might be to start fresh.

"Let's tackle this from the perspective of tabula rosa," De Luca stated.

She asked Veronica to develop the next year's marketing plan as well as an operations plan and public relations strategy.

De Luca reminded Veronica that if she was not going to work according to her plan and her direction, it would be the best for all concerned that they let her go.

Taylor Davidson was first and foremost a bottom-feeding prick. Veronica referred to him as "not so tricky prick," a play on words version of "tricky dick," a term that had gained popularity as a nickname for Richard Nixon.

Davidson fancied himself as being shrewd and calculating, when in fact he was neither. He simply wanted to control everything.

Veronica was the only one who was not afraid for her job, the only one who was not afraid to stand up to him.

Davidson wanted her to go. He told her in no uncertain terms that she was a threat to him, because she knew how to run a business, knew marketing, and put up resistance to everything he wanted.

Veronica was able to defend her professional opinions with intelligence and business savvy. Davidson possessed neither quality, so opted for a rawer and eviler plan of action. He would attack her personally.

Davidson became friendly with some of the staff, going out drinking with them on a regular basis. He would even invite Veronica out for drinks after telling her to fuck off.

There was another director at the community named Jansen Martin with whom Davidson became increasingly chummy. There was an undeniable attraction between Jansen and Veronica from the moment they met, but Veronica was certainly not going to act upon it.

Davidson must have noticed the chemistry between the two, and that became the genesis of the plan he devised with Jansen. In a move most evil and despicable, Jansen would pursue her romantically.

Jansen texted her and hit on her constantly, professing to her that she was his soul mate. He was married, but he told Veronica he and his wife were separated, and they had filed for divorce.

Eventually Jansen and Veronica did begin to date, albeit very casually. They went out for lunch, went for the occasional drive after work. They kissed and made out lightly, nothing ever more than that. Their relationship lasted about four months.

Veronica seriously questioned their relationship, however. She asked Jansen repeatedly why they never went out publicly or why there never seemed to be any progress with his divorce. Jansen shirked the questions off, never responding with anything remotely resembling a concrete answer and instead would state, "I'm gonna marry you, babe. Just be patient. You are my soul mate."

Upon finding out that Jansen was not getting divorced and he had been seeing another girl, Veronica confronted him.

Jansen said, "I am leaving my wife, Veronica, but for my real soul mate who is already living with me."

Jansen threw major damage Veronica's way by telling her he was going to be with another woman. Veronica felt used and humiliated, like she was the brunt of a huge cosmic joke. It was devious and disgusting, and she was leveled by it—literally brought to her knees.

The attack by Taylor Davidson was professional, psychological, romantic, and now personal.

Veronica remained at the community organization for another three months, during which time she began laying the foundation for starting her own company. She had always wanted to own a marketing firm, so she was going to go for it.

Her experiences with the Tennessee community had taught her that she really did know more about marketing, sales, public relations, communications, accounting, and operations than the majority of people she worked with or for did.

She decided to call her business Veritas Group Marketing (VGM). She chose Veritas because she loved the meaning—truth. In Roman mythology, Veritas was the daughter of Saturn and the mother of Virtue. After her traumatic experiences at the community, the idea of forthright truth just felt right.

And she definitely wanted to use the letter *V* in the company name. Once at a post office Veronica was required to sign for some packages. The postal worker told her that she analyzed handwriting prior to her work with the postal services, and she could tell by the way she made her *V* that Veronica was destined for success in a small town.

Veronica appreciated the prediction of success but could not fathom being stuck in a small town.

VGM was success bound almost from the moment Veronica started it. As she was able to conduct the majority of VGM business remotely, she bought a house in Little Rock, Arkansas, where she could run her business and enjoy being closer to her parents.

Chapter 10

Sociopathic Liar

Veronica's company was successful, but she was not at the best place personally in her life. She had post-traumatic stress from her experience with Taylor Davidson and Jansen.

It was still hard for her to process, hard to even put into words how horribly she had been treated. The pure evil and deliberate cruelty were hard to fathom. She read and committed to memory a famous quote of Tennessee Williams made more famous by Blanche DuBois. "Some things are not forgivable. Deliberate cruelty is not forgivable. It is the one unforgivable thing in my opinion, and the one thing of which I have never, ever been guilty."

Veronica's sister Mia knew that Veronica was in a bad place emotionally, and she thought that a shiny new man in her life might put the spark back in Veronica's eyes. Mia suggested dating apps.

The first man that Veronica met was Ethan Markham. In his bio, he stated that he was a twice-divorced dad of three amazing children, and he was looking for a committed relationship. He valued the principles of honesty, respect, and compatibility. He added that he would view the woman who became his romantic partner as a complete equal in all aspects of life—but that he still believed in chivalry, and he had to admit that he would treat her like a queen.

Veronica was genuinely curious and interested enough to pursue a date with him but knew that she was still raw from the Taylor/ Jansen betrayal.

Ethan, on the other hand, was very enthusiastic and began calling Veronica every day. They talked a few hours each night. After three weeks, they met for coffee, and true to his bio, he seemed both genuine and chivalrous.

After coffee and bagels, they went for a long walk and savored the delightful weather. When it was time to go, he asked her if he could kiss her. It was a sweet kiss, and Veronica found it charming that he asked.

The following week they had their second date. Ethan came to her place. They dined on a special dinner he brought, watched a movie, and fooled around a little bit.

On the third date, Ethan came over again. They worked together in the kitchen as they prepared a delicious dinner, followed by equally delicious sex. So began the beginning of an actual relationship, the first one for Veronica in a while. Ethan spoke proudly about his children, and Veronica completely understood his need to take time before introducing her.

The relationship progressed nicely, at a pleasant and unhurried pace. They had many things in common. They enjoyed movies, traveling, taking leisurely walks, and appreciating the beauty of nature, and they both loved animals. Their conversations never hit lulls as they always found things to talk about.

There were some distinct differences, though. Veronica was a city girl. Ethan was born rural, and though he had traveled, he was definitely a country boy, an Arkansas boy. He had a farm complete with goats, chickens, and horses. Visiting him at his farm brought back sweet and nostalgic memories of Veronica's summer trips to Oklahoma.

First, she met Ethan's son Caleb, who was twelve. A few weeks later, she met Connor, fourteen. Both boys were from Ethan's first marriage.

Veronica developed an easy and close rapport with the boys quickly, and even accompanied Ethan to their football games. She took them school shopping, and she, Ethan, and the boys would spend holidays at Ethan's parents' home as well as at her parents.'

Several months later Veronica met Ethan's daughter Marie, who lived with her mother out of state. Marie was Ethan's daughter from his second marriage. She had come to spend a week with Ethan during spring break.

Marie was a sweet, but reserved girl, not as extroverted as her half-brothers were. She was eight years old and was beginning to show signs of body image issues.

Observing Marie's unease with her body and general lack of self-confidence caused Veronica to reflect on how difficult it was for girls to navigate life in a world of airbrushed images of perfection and unrealistic and often unattainable, standards of femininity and beauty.

She hoped that Marie would develop enough trust in her to view her as a positive role model. She wanted to help Marie understand that intelligence, financial independence, and self-confidence were more important than a dress size.

Ethan shared with Veronica that Marie was having difficulty accepting the fact that her parents' marriage was over. Veronica and Ethan discussed the possibility of him visiting Marie in Florida more often, perhaps even taking the opportunity to speak with some of her teachers. Veronica thought it was a great idea and did not hesitate to offer Ethan her complete support.

Several weeks later Ethan went to visit Marie in Florida. At this point Veronica and Ethan were a year and a half into their relationship. They were not living together, but would text each other frequently throughout the day, especially when they were apart, or if anything major happened in either of their lives. They always spoke at night. It was part of their informal couple's code of conduct. It was important to Ethan; he considered it open communication, directly related to one of his principles—honesty.

On this particular trip, Ethan suddenly stopped responding to Veronica's texts. She also tried calling him but had to leave phone messages because he never answered her calls.

About a week later, he texted Veronica, offering an apology and an explanation: "So sorry, my love, that I have not responded. I really have no excuse, but I do have an explanation. There has been so much going on with Marie. I have met with her teachers and the guidance counselor. You met her; I am sure you could tell that she needs a lot of attention. I still should have made time to text you, I know. I guess worrying about Marie depleted my energy. Please forgive me. I love you."

Veronica did forgive Ethan, but her forgiveness did not come without much thought and contemplation of what had happened. After all, she had spent the entire week worrying if everything was okay. *Had he been in an accident? Did something happen to Marie?*

Ethan and Veronica got back on track, and everything was smooth sailing for the next several months. Ethan had been building a home for a few years and had talked about it when he and Veronica had first met. He brought Veronica over once a month to see his progress and for design advice.

When he was very close to completion and working on final changes like interior doors, cabinet hardware, and paint colors, Veronica hosted a housewarming party for Ethan and the boys. She invited both families, surrounding neighbors, and some of Ethan's coworkers. Ethan was very appreciative, and the boys seemed very happy. It was one of those occasions when Veronica could actually see them living together and being a family. Sure, there were some difficulties surrounding Marie, but Veronica felt they could overcome them.

Ethan and Veronica continued to become more invested as a couple. They all went to farm auctions together, and when Ethan traveled for

IT work to Brazil, Mexico, Australia, and other exotic locales, he brought her back a special gift. He invited her each time he traveled, but she could not go except for a few sexy, fun weekend getaways to New York City. As a new business owner, she just couldn't spend too much time away from her business.

Veronica did join Ethan on a trip to San Francisco where they had a lot to drink, had a fight, and words were spoken. They talked about their future and marriage, and Veronica got pissed when she thought he said, "I've decided not to get married." That was definitely not something Veronica wanted to hear. They both decided to let it go, as they had a lot to drink and called it a night.

The following morning was full of sunshine, blue skies, and billowy San Francisco breezes. Ethan and Veronica decided to forget the things that were said the previous night. They were drunk, and it was their vacation. They went on to have a fun day sightseeing including seeing the spectacular redwood trees and whale watching.

Ethan was definitely a romantic and compassionate man with a sentimental heart. When Veronica's sweet foster dog Binky passed away suddenly, he helped her find a new puppy that the boys named Ruger.

And when Veronica decided she wanted another dog so that Ruger would have a companion, Ethan bought her a dog the boys named Beretta. Veronica would bring Ruger and Beretta to Ethan's, and the dogs would run on the farm. All of them would play catch and football and have a great time together as a couple and as a family.

Every other holiday, Ethan would go to Florida to see Marie. Ethan's ex-wife Priscilla had a very small apartment, so Ethan, Priscilla, and Marie would stay in a hotel to all be together. Veronica let him know that she was not comfortable with him staying in the same hotel with his ex-wife.

Ethan would reassure Veronica that they always got separate, adjoining rooms, with Priscilla and Marie in one room and Ethan in the other. He encouraged Veronica to understand, pleading that it was the best arrangement he could make in order to see Marie. "She is making such progress, Veronica," Ethan told her repeatedly.

As the owner of her own marketing company, Veronica was naturally always on social media. She repeatedly asked Ethan why he did not post anything about them on Facebook. They had taken many pictures of them as a couple and of them with the kids.

Ethan would repeat that he was locked out of Facebook because he forgot his password. Veronica offered to help him resolve the situation, but Ethan would tell her not to worry and that he would figure it out.

One day Veronica was surprised to see a new friend request from Ethan Markham. She texted him and asked him what was going on.

"I just started a new Facebook page as it was too frustrating with the other one," Ethan texted. "You will be my first friend," Ethan continued.

Veronica was pleased, but a week passed, and she thought it strange that Ethan still only had one friend—Veronica. She also noticed that her posts to him seemed to disappear shortly after she posted them. And when she had shared or posted photos of them, they also seemed to disappear immediately.

When she asked Ethan about it, he feigned ignorance. "I don't know, Veronica. I have always had trouble with this social media crap."

Veronica reminded him again that she could help him. She was taken back when Ethan replied, "It's just Facebook, Veronica. Please quit nagging me about it."

She let the comment roll off her back, attributing it to his stress about Marie.

A week later, Ethan went to a trap shoot competition with Caleb, Connor, and his dad. Veronica was to accompany them but could not go due to work, so she called to see if they had fun and how they had fared in the competition. Ethan called her back forty-five minutes later and said she was very harassing and that he needed a break.

Then Ethan called her back again and apologized. "I'm just stressed, babe," he said. "I'm sorry. They tell you being a parent is hard, but sometimes, it goes way beyond that. I love you so much."

Veronica said she understood.

Two weeks later, he called her and said, "This isn't working for me."

The next morning, he texted her and said, "I cannot live without you. My mind is racing. Priscilla is dating and being completely irresponsible causing Marie to miss school almost three times a week, and my God, she is only eight."

Veronica texted back that she understood, but she could not help but think that Ethan was heading for a nervous breakdown.

When Ethan returned from another trip to Florida, there was a lot of tension, and they had constant fights. So, when Ethan had to go to DC for business, Veronica was actually looking forward to some alone time. When he returned from DC, things seemed fine for a few days.

Ethan typically went to Veronica's events with her, and he had planned to attend an awards gala, but he canceled at the last minute. Veronica was hurt and frustrated, she was literally sick to her stomach from it all. She decided she was not in the mood for anything festive or celebratory, so she did not attend the event either. Later that night, she learned she had won the Entrepreneur of the Year award.

Damn him, Veronica thought. *I missed awesomeness!*

My Heart Hurts

Ethan began experiencing health problems that were eventually determined to be symptomatic of a genetic heart problem. Surgery was scheduled in Little Rock. Priscilla and Marie flew down, and Veronica took them to dinner.

The surgery was successful, and Ethan was expected to make a full recovery. Veronica drove him home after the surgery. She helped console the kids and made sure Ethan had everything he needed over the next several months.

Veronica noticed that Ethan was spending a lot of time texting Priscilla and speaking to her on the phone. She expressed her concerns on more than one occasion, and Ethan always had an explanation. He claimed Priscilla was trying to sue him, that she overdrew their account, or that Marie was upset again, and she needed his help. The list of scenarios and explanations seemed endless.

Veronica initiated a conversation with Ethan about her concerns with their relationship, and to her surprise, Ethan seemed candid and willing to address the issues that troubled her.

Ethan was laid off from work, and they made a decision to spend a few days in Nashville to reignite their relationship. Veronica did all the planning and prepaid the trip. She and Ethan thought the time away would get them back on track romantically and give Ethan some clarity and focus. When they returned, he would direct his energy toward finding a new job.

Two days before they were scheduled to leave, Ethan said he was not going to go, that he needed to see Marie, causing Veronica heartache and financial loss. He said Marie was experiencing fear and anxiety over Ethan's recent health concerns. Veronica was beyond frustrated, but she understood the situation from the little girl's perspective. It was frightening to think that your father might die suddenly.

Weeks later, they had plans for Memorial Day. They were hosting a cookout and then attending a concert. All systems were a go. Everything was in place, except for Ethan. He simply did not show up.

Veronica texted him, "Are you still coming over?"

Ethan texted back a response saying he was drunk and depressed, adding, "I am going to disappear for a while, just give me a month or two or three, then we will be back together."

Veronica did not need to think twice before responding, "No. Fuck you. We are done." She felt that she had put up with more than enough. Ethan was inconsiderate, unreliable, and a user.

A month later, Veronica was curious and checked Ethan's Facebook page. There were considerably more posts than the last time Veronica had visited. The first one she read was one from Priscilla— "I am so happy to be living with my husband again."

What the hell? Veronica thought.

Then she saw numerous posts from Priscilla's friends congratulating them. "So glad you are back together." "The perfect couple, a couple again," and "We knew you would work it out." Perhaps the most startling post was from Ethan, "We were never divorced, just separated. Now we are rekindling our marriage. And we are taking a getaway, just the two of us... to Nashville."

Tears of frustration, anger, and hurt were streaming down Veronica's cheeks as she began deleting all social media contact with Ethan, including his sons, mom, and sister, who loved Veronica and continued to like each of her posts.

As she was preparing to "unfriend" Connor, she got a text from him. "You were the best thing that ever happened to my dad. My brother and I did not know he was still married. Thank you for being so nice to us."

In that moment, Veronica realized the depth of Ethan's deceit. If his kids did not know, certainly his parents must not have known either.

Veronica reviewed every interaction with Ethan, each time they were together, all the texts and phone calls that did not make sense. The times they would stay in hotels because of Priscilla's tiny apartment.

Veronica concluded that Ethan was just looking for a bitch slave to take care of his kids, cook, and clean. So many lies, a web of sociopathic deceit. What was so extraordinarily painful was the timing of Ethan's psychopathic behavior. He came into her life right after Veronica's dealings with Taylor Davidson and Jansen Martin. She was beginning to wonder if she would ever find happiness with a man—if she could ever trust again.

She also questioned her abilities as an empath. Where was her radar, her early warning system? Veronica realized that if she was to be brutally honest with herself, there were inklings of trouble and many dreams that were cautionary. But Veronica made decisions repeatedly, to drown out the voices, to ignore the inner warnings.

Perhaps it was because there were children involved, or perhaps it was because she just could not fathom or deal with back-to-back treachery having just endured the horrible experience with Jansen.

Veronica found out sometime later from his sister that Ethan had lost another job, and that he, Priscilla, and the kids were living in a tempo-rary trailer with most of Veronica's gifts and loaned furniture.

A year or so later, on one random day, Ethan reached out to her and asked if she would like to try again. *Dumb ass.* For once, when Veronica thought about Ethan, she actually laughed.

Chapter 11

Heart Repair

After Veronica's breakup with Ethan, she decided to focus any free time she had on her home. She wanted to make some improvements, and she needed the services of a contractor.

A colleague introduced her to a SWAT instructor named Jacob who was looking for part-time contract work when in the Little Rock area. There was an instant attraction that started a fun flirtation between them.

A friend named Matt came with Jacob, and the afternoon after he and Jacob left, Matt sent Veronica pictures of naked women, big dick jokes, and other typical fare that kids found humorous.

Jacob called her to schedule a time to return with estimates, and Veronica asked him to tell Matt that the jokes were not cool.

"It just makes me feel uncomfortable," Veronica said. "If he was coming on to me, I certainly do not want to encourage it."

Jacob told her he would speak to Matt, and he apologized for Matt making her feel uncomfortable.

True Love

Jacob came over with the estimates, and Veronica was very pleased that the costs were much less than she expected. The two continued their flirtatious dance—laughing at jokes that probably were not that funny, making double entendres amid hair tosses, and sucking in abs when the other was not looking.

"You know," Veronica said in a voice that was half-cool girl and half coo, "I really appreciate you making the time to work on my house. Especially since you have such a demanding, high-pressure job and are only in the area for short periods."

Jacob smiled that warm, boyish, yet knowing, masculine smile she had come to savor in just two short meetings and thanked her.

"Honestly, if everyone was as nice as you, I would accept more contract work," Jacob replied. "I already ordered some of the supplies I will need to get started from a fixtures and restoration shop about seven miles from here. They will be ready for me to pick up tomorrow afternoon. Then I can get started next week."

After contemplating her next move for a few seconds, Veronica thought she should just go for it. "Since you are coming out this way tomorrow, why don't you stop by after picking up the supplies? I can make us dinner. It's my way of saying thank you for making home improvement affordable for a single, working woman."

Veronica was very pleased he accepted her invitation. Jacob was very handsome, and he seemed so down to earth, genuine, and kind. She really needed to be in the company of decent men, even if he was a relative stranger, she enjoyed flirting with. She needed to know good guys still existed.

Jacob came for dinner as planned, complete with fresh flowers and a bottle of wine. Veronica prepared lasagna, thinking it would be a good choice since she could prepare it ahead of time.

She tossed a fresh green salad and bought some sourdough rolls that she brushed with olive oil, basil, and oregano. Dessert was vanilla ice cream, topped with a generous pouring of Kahlúa.

They had a wonderful time. Dinner was delicious. Veronica and Jacob laughed and shared their basic life stories.

Jacob was a SWAT team director turned instructor based in Memphis, but he traveled throughout Arkansas and frequently throughout the southern part of the country as well. He was divorced with no kids.

Veronica gave him the highlights of her life. She spoke a bit about some of the heartbreaks and betrayals. She hadn't planned to, but they were parts of her life. As she spoke, she realized that was exactly what they were—fragments that were parts of the essence of Veronica. They were glass shards of a grand mosaic. Sure, some were larger and had sharper edges that could pierce flesh, but they were surrounded by pieces of multicolored glass that looked like precious stones. Precious stones with perfectly rounded edges that were as impenetrable as they were smooth. *Every stone I have ever picked up by the water has been smooth.*

"Hey, where did you go just now?" Jacob said, gently guiding her out of her moment of reflection.

"Just thinking about stones," Veronica said. "When you pick up a stone and skim it across the water, the stone touches the surface of the water, and ripples from that get larger and larger, all from skimming a stone across the water."

"Hmm, when I take my fishing boat out in the water, the engine causes ripples, too," Jacob added.

Veronica loved the look on his face. It was precious. It was the look of a little boy trying to add something big to a conversation.

They looked at each other and then burst into laughter. Then they found lighthearted movies to watch on television while kissing and snuggling.

Jacob came back for a second date the next time he was in town. They ordered pizza and polished off two bottles of wine. This time they graduated from the heavy petting to sex.

He gave her oral sex, and it was the first time in her life she ever enjoyed it with a man. It was the first time in her life it was not marred by images of abuse from the past. It was... magical.

They began a romantic relationship. They laughed. They talked. The communication was easy and effortless. He did not merely understand her. He got her.

They had sex in random places when he was in town. Veronica felt that the sex with him was amazing. He took the time to know her body, inside and out, a true connection of two souls.

Jacob was a good, solid man. He was respectful of Veronica. He was nonjudgmental of her opinions, her experiences, and her dreams for the future.

Since his job required a lot of travel, often he was gone for months at a time. But he made the effort to ensure she knew he loved her unconditionally. She loved him.

While Jacob could not imagine a world without her, he had a hard time imagining things going on this way forever. He wanted more, but his travels changed territories.

So, they decided to remain great friends. Veronica was more hopeful, more grateful, perhaps a bit less world weary, because she had met Jacob. He had become a part of her life. The ripple effects he caused were large and far-reaching.

He sent her flowers a month or so after their romance ended. The card attached read, "Just so you know, I will love you always."

Do the Twist

Veronica and her mom took a mini vacation to Tampa. It was a great trip; she spent time with Yvonne and Scarlett.

Pleasantly exhausted from the sun and the beach one day, Veronica went to sleep but woke up in the middle of the night from her back cracking and popping. She felt and heard it.

She attributed it to fatigue and possibly an overzealous stretch. Whatever it was, it did not prevent her from falling back asleep.

She woke up in the morning and was still in pain. She bought some over-the-counter mentholated rub to ease the pain. It helped a bit, but she still had great discomfort. It was certainly not enough to prevent her from enjoying the remainder of her vacation, though. Tenacious Veronica.

When they got back home, she went to a chiropractor a few days a week for over a month, and it eased the pain some.

Then one day, Veronica went on a photo shoot for a big client of VGM and found herself in weird contortions and positions trying to set up the perfect angle to take the perfect photograph.

The pain after the photo shoot was insufferable and was no longer just in her back. It spread to the left hip, right hip, right leg, and right ankle.

From X-rays to MRIs, CTs, and hospital trips, no one could identify what was causing her pain, so she was referred to physical therapy for six weeks. It did not help, and she started to feel like her whole body was out of alignment. She needed to take over-the-counter pain medications and creams to get through each day.

Thus, began an eighteen-month process of seeing different physicians and specialists. This included a neurosurgeon, orthopedic surgeon, and more.

Frustrated and suffering, Veronica did a lot of research and felt strongly that she may have suffered a pinched nerve, something she had suspected for a while, but the doctors kept rebuffing her theory.

She returned to her neurosurgeon, and they discussed her research, symptoms, and her sense of what was going on with her body. He performed

a myelogram to get a better image of her back and a subsequent nerve con-
ductor test, which showed problems with the L5 and S1 areas.

Chapter 12

Stealing Oxygen

Since leaving the international escapade of Barcelona, the cultural wonderland that was New York City, and the mixed bag of fun, sun, and drama of Tampa, so much had happened to Veronica.

After the demoralizing mind-screw perpetrated against her by Taylor Davidson and his crony Jansen Martin, followed by the ongoing epic lies of Ethan Markham, there was the passionate, almost redemptive love of Jacob.

Veronica was now experiencing what it was like to put down roots. She loved her home in Little Rock. She loved living near her parents and relished the opportunity to get to know them as people.

Her company, VGM, was growing with an impressive mix of clients, and Veronica felt financially secure.

Dating after forty-five, however, was a shit show. Little Rock definitely had some big-city attributes, but Arkansas life overall moved at a much slower pace. Most people Veronica's age married right after high school, started their families, and by age thirty-five were settled in and comfortable with their lot in life.

Married men hit on Veronica all the time. It was awkward and uncomfortable as she knew the wives of many of them. Some of the men were even employees of clients.

Veronica took a giant leap of faith after meeting Ethan Markham on Tinder and tried the site again. She also tried Bumble. Her experience was that the men she met on these apps were just looking for hookups.

Veronica remembered one instance when a man she had met on Bumble texted her to say he would be a little late for their planned date. She waited forty-five minutes then left. He texted her again after two and a half hours, asking her for her address, stating that he would just come to her house instead to have fun. Veronica promptly texted an emphatic, "Hell no!" She could not believe any man worth spending any time with would suggest anything so unsafe.

Throughout her life, Veronica remained deeply attuned to her empathic powers and her intuition. They were part of what made her uniquely her. When she sketched and meditated, it brought the feelings associated with her special powers closer to the surface and made them easier to identify.

She began journaling after her move to Little Rock, partly because it was a way of dealing with stressors. But also, because she had seen so many beautiful places in her life and had had so many wild and unique experiences. She had met and known such a diverse group of people—had such highs and had experienced many lows—and she did not want to take the chance that she would forget any of it.

Veronica had a kind heart and a compassionate nature, and when she became friends with someone, she was a true friend. She was the proverbial shoulder to cry on, the woman who took your phone call at 3:00 a.m. or brought you bourbon and expensive dark chocolate when you needed a good friend and a stiff drink.

But genuine true friendships had eluded Veronica most of her life. Most were what she called "broken birds," people who needed to be fixed or healed and were not interested in contributing anything to the relationship.

So, it was not happenstance that some of her first journaling entries were about these takers.

One of those friendships was with a woman named Sabrina. Sabrina was a massage therapist who was chronically fearful that her husband would cheat on her. This fear was the primary focal point of conversation between Veronica and Sabrina. In fact, when Veronica would shift the focus of conversation to her own feelings and needs, Sabrina would belittle her feelings and interject that her life and her issues should take center stage.

Veronica knew that Sabrina was very competitive and jealous of her. She remembered when Sabrina had expressed—no, seethed—resentment at the number of suitors pursuing Veronica and stated clearly that Veronica did not deserve all that male attention. "I deserve to be pursued like that. It should be me!" she had exclaimed.

The final and fatal blow had occurred when Veronica paid Sabrina to give Miguel a massage. His muscles were overextended and sore from rugby, and Veronica thought it would be a nice treat, especially since it was not something, he would plan to do for himself.

A day after the massage, Sabrina told Veronica that Miguel seemed to enjoy his massage and that they talked about nothing in particular during the session, just the friendly small talk that she and clients typically engaged in. But she made a point to express how aroused he was by her.

When Veronica asked Miguel if he enjoyed the massage, he could not wait to share. He told her he had felt extremely uncomfortable as Sabrina hit on him the entire time.

"I spoke about you nonstop because, well, you happen to be one of my favorite topics." Miguel winked at Veronica as he continued, "But she just kept changing the subject and flirting. I could not help but wonder why you consider her to be a friend."

Upon reflection after that comment, she realized every time Sabrina gave her a massage, Veronica felt her energy being completely drained from her body. It was as if she had received a transfusion and all her positive energy and healing breaths were replaced with toxic, choking half breaths. Veronica also remembered that she always seemed to literally get sick after one of Sabrina's massages.

Conversely, Sabrina would always comment that Veronica gave her a sense of elation, like a three-day high. Those distinctly different emotions and experiences really summed up the rhythm of their relationship. Sabrina sucked Veronica's energy.

That next day Veronica called Sabrina with the intent of meeting her for a drink to tell her the friendship wasn't working. Sabrina did not answer, and Veronica left a message extending an invitation for a glass of wine that evening.

Sabrina returned her call within five minutes, her voice frantic. "Oh my God, Veronica, your message, you sounded so distressed. Were you trying to upset me?"

Veronica responded immediately, "Seriously, you think I sounded distressed, and it doesn't occur to you to ask if I am okay, if something is going on with me? You immediately think only of yourself." She continued, "You steal my energy. You are jealous, always in competition with me. I wish you no ill will; we just are no longer friends."

Belittled and Insulted

Jacqueline was another woman Veronica knew when she lived in both Galveston and New York City. Jacqueline called Veronica almost nightly for advice with her love life.

When Jacqueline talked, Veronica listened. When Jacqueline cried, which was often, Veronica held her hand.

Like her relationship with Sabrina, if Veronica shared her feelings or frustrations with Jacqueline, she made it known that she found Veronica's problems annoying and insignificant in comparison to hers.

Jacqueline may have had legitimate issues in her love life, but Veronica had always managed to work full-time in stressful business environments that required frequent travel, and she had some PTSD from events in her life. Veronica had real issues that should elicit a feeling of concern and comforting actions from a sincere friend.

Several times in her life when Veronica endured health concerns, she called Jacqueline for support. Jacqueline's response was always the same. She was simply too busy. Veronica knew she could certainly always rely on Miguel, but Jacqueline's indifference hurt her deeply.

Once when Veronica was on a business trip in Vegas, Jacqueline had come along for fun. Veronica met her for drinks at a bar after work. Jacqueline was in rare form taking the opportunity to insult Veronica publicly every opportunity she had. Veronica had grown weary of Jacqueline's verbal punches and asked her to leave. Jacqueline's response had been that it was time to divorce their friendship of many years. Veronica did not argue.

Veronica wrote many journal entries about relationships like the ones with Jacqueline and Sabrina, in addition to ones about her issues with her now chronic back pain.

Veronica was in physical and emotional pain most of her life caused, in equal parts, by health issues and thoughtless men and women. And when she committed those thoughts to paper, it brought tears to her eyes.

Surprisingly, Veronica did not get angry when she read her accounts of her relationships with these broken birds, oxygen suckers, users, cheaters, and liars. She felt wiser and more aware of the type of people she wanted in her life circle.

Self-Actualized Peace

Veronica's life was a full one. Being a business owner kept her busy and being a pet parent to her sweet furry friends kept her happy. Despite her health woes and emotional blows, Veronica remained an optimist with a positive personality and upbeat attitude. She may have been broken in places, but she was still strong.

Her mother asked her throughout her adult life how she could live with pain, discomfort, and the uncertainty of the cause of that pain and remain upbeat and energetic. Veronica's response was always that she had to. "Gotta keep keeping on, Mom," she would say.

Laura Mitchell once sent a card to Veronica that she keeps to this day. "Darling, you are very strong and always have been. No one else could handle all you have lived with and remain so cheerful and giving through it all."

The truth was Veronica sometimes felt worn down, but she was able to muster her strength and pursue her goals. She was tired but serene. She often preferred to be alone but could be the bright spot in any room when needed. She was a caretaker, a healer, and an exceptionally compassionate person.

Veronica smiled as she thought of all the bars, clubs, and restaurants she had closed down in her life... some of the best in the world. Looking around her cozy and inviting home, she marveled at how different her current life in Little Rock looked.

Bedtime was definitely coming a lot earlier! This was also the first time since she was a teen that she was not involved with a man in some way. There currently was no lover, boyfriend, boy toy, or friend with benefits. She was truly single. No drama. No attachment. No heartbreak. No bullshit. And she was not lonely.

For the first time in her life, Veronica realized that solitude wasn't just free time in between commitments or scheduled events. Nor did it have to mean emptiness.

For Veronica Mitchell solitude meant a vast open space where she could create any landscape that pleased her. It meant peace.

She was grateful that the always dashing and debonair Garit was still her friend. And her soul mate Miguel, now living in Chicago, was still in her life, although he did end up getting married twice.

His family introduced him to a Venezuelan woman that fit the bill for the wife he now desired. Veronica felt like her heart had been pierced when she heard the marriage news again, but they were still great friends. They were forever Veronica and Miguel.

She sometimes believed that God forgot to create a husband for her in this life or that the husband-to-be turned gay.

She made peace with the possibility that she may be alone the rest of her life with a possible lover now and again. She just prayed she would have someone kind and trustworthy by her side, lover or friend, when her parents' health declined, and they passed on.

She feared that would be the hardest time of her life, and that despite everything she had been through, she would not be able to handle it alone.

Curse Lifted

On a particularly beautiful autumn day in Little Rock, Veronica completed a journal entry, responded to some VGM emails, and set out to run some errands. She parked her car and walked to the farmers' market.

She noticed a psychic had a booth set up between the peaches and the jars of canned preserves and peanut brittle.

"What the heck?" she said to herself as she walked over, sat down, and handed over her twenty dollars.

After the woman with a Jamaican accent who identified herself as Mabel gave some generic insights, she asked Veronica if she had a childhood friend named Alyson. "No," Veronica responded, "but I did have a friend named Amanda."

"Cursed," Mabel responded.

"I beg your pardon?" Veronica asked.

"This Amanda put a curse on you. You will not have children. You will not find lasting love. All because she feels you abandoned her."

Veronica silently stared at Mabel for what felt like an eternity but was in fact only a few moments.

"Did you hear me, miss?" Mabel asked.

"Yes, thank you, have a good day," Veronica said as she gathered her purse and walked off quickly.

She had a meeting with one of her staff in two hours. She reached into her purse for her phone and texted that she needed to reschedule the meeting. Veronica needed to walk, needed to think. She needed to process what Mabel had told her.

Obviously, she did not and would not have children. The necessary hysterectomy had taken care of that. And, while she had known true love, she had not known lasting love.

Maybe she would get married and know and hold on to lasting love. That was, she guessed, yet to be determined.

What Veronica Mitchell could not escape, on this otherwise spec-tacular fall day, was the fact that Mabel was the sixth psychic who had identified her childhood friend Amanda as having cursed her. Veronica sipped her coffee and walked past the trendy boutiques and funky, artsy specialty shops. She took a big gulp of her coffee and realized her cup was almost empty.

But my cup has always runneth over, a voice from within her protested.

She stared at the store windows on both sides of her, searching for a coffee shop or bistro, thinking inexplicably that extra caffeine could calm her down.

Pausing when she noticed a boutique with signs advertising cappuc-cino and frozen lattes, she decided to walk in.

Her eyes immediately locked with a man who looked up from the selection of food he was perusing. She remembered the time she and Miguel had locked eyes in Cádiz.

Deciding she really did not need the latte, she left the store and continued down the street, stopping in front of a home renovation store. Walking in, she was taken back by how beautiful the kitchen displays were. One in particular reminded her of the home that Robbie had bought in Dallas, the home he wanted her to live in with him as his wife.

Almost near the side street where she had parked her car, she crossed and noticed a comic store. Large posters in the window advertised SWAT and undercover brothers of war comics, and a picture of Jacob came to mind.

Veronica's thoughts were interrupted by her vibrating phone. The number did not look readily familiar, but she recognized the voice offering the warm greeting as a potential client, referred by an existing client.

"Hey, Tanya," Veronica said, happy for the distraction.

"Hi, Veronica. I absolutely am thrilled to say that I am looking forward to becoming a client of VGM. As my mama would say, I know you'll do me proud."

"That's great, Tanya. Welcome to VGM. When I get back to the office, I'll check my calendar, and I'll call you to schedule a time to meet to plan our strategy."

The two women exchanged fond farewells, and Veronica continued toward her car. She walked by the right side of the farmers' market and saw a cluster of the vendors chatting as they surveyed the patrons walking by the booths.

Suddenly, she saw the figure of a woman dressed in bright and festive clothing emerge from the center of the market. The woman removed her sunglasses, and Veronica instantly recognized her as the psychic Mabel.

Mabel turned, and spotting Veronica, she kept her gaze on her as she walked. The expression on Mabel's face was serious. Veronica kept looking straight ahead but shifted her eyes to the left once, in time to see Mabel shaking her head slowly. Veronica was able to read Mabel's lips as she moved them in exaggerated fashion. "But the curse has been lifted."

Veronica clicked her car key chain and heard the doors unlock. She opened the door and eased into her Lexus.

Then the phone rang. It was Jacob. He found a new job near her. After telling her all about the new position, he paused briefly and then asked, "Will you marry me?"